I0764394

# MILITARY ROADS

*Also by John Fraser*
*and published by AESOP Modern Fiction:*

Animal Tales
Black Masks
Blue Light / Starting Over
The Case
Down from the Stars
Enterprising Women
Hard Places
An Illusion of Sun
The Magnificent Wurlitzer
Medusa
The Observatory
The Other Shore
The Red Tank
Runners
Soft Landing
The Storm
Three Beauties
Wayfaring

# MILITARY ROADS

John Fraser

AESOP Modern Fiction
Oxford

AESOP Modern Fiction
An imprint of AESOP Publications
Martin Noble Editorial / AESOP
28a Abberbury Road, Oxford OX4 4ES, UK
www.aseopbooks.com

First edition published by AESOP Publications

www.johnfraserfiction.com



A catalogue record of this book is available from the British Library.

First edition 2012, revised 2024



ISBN: 978-0-9569098-6-2

# Contents

# Hunting

Da brennt ihre Fahne mitten im Feind, und sie jagen ihr nach.*

Rainer Maria Rilke, *Die Weise von Liebe und Tod des Cornets Christopher Rilke*

THE DUNES stroll away like waves of the yellow sea.

My friend – Finch, we call him – has made a cityscape. It fills this little house – more like a shack. The room – could be a street in some Soho, London, New York, miniature, quite personal. He adds a small restored Colosseum, statue of the Colossus too – him, Finch, in his country clothes. On the sidewalks, blobby replicas of us, his friends. Friends of his, of our, youth:

Dea, the joyous, uninvited friend of life. Mansour, forever destitute, unaccepting of poverty as his destiny. Luca, the pure but not especially noble soul – slave to old books. Odile, mundane, untrusting, in a set of mismatched clothes. The women, naturally, more

* Their banner is burning in the midst of the enemy, and they ride after it.

beautiful, desirable, than now. Myself – between experiences, then as now.

There's other friends as well, no family, though Finch gets his power from relatives – this little country, just a hop across the sea from us, is almost his, there to pick up like a fallen fruit of good or evil – and we drop in when driven or when bored. Finch. Friend.

The miniature fills the only room, alcoves left for sleeping in, if the mood takes hold of you. Outside, the sand.

'It's to avoid nostalgia, this mock-up,' he says. 'See, you're all there, quite small. Just like real city life.'

I say, 'You could have stayed back there and seen us life-size every day.'

He pushes me out back – 'There is a cat. Quite desperate. There's lots of sand here, as you see, but not a lot to eat. I can't meet all its needs,' and he points around – there's not much here. We don't see the cat.

'The locals think a pet's a stupid luxury,' he says, 'You'll see, there's no rats here.'

I say, 'The locals seem to draw too fine a point.' At this, he nods.

'It's all memory,' he says, 'And yes, it's all a little false. All there even when you don't want to remember. Or can't.'

I say, 'You don't seem to have much time for us, individually. It's just a made-up scene. You might add figurines of people who you've never met,' and he says,

'Yes! I might. This here, though, is all my living space. And friends – well, you need this little lump of them to fill a little section of your life. See – here's the bar, that guy was shot there for bad debts. We didn't drink there, after. Superstition! Whores lived here,' he points, and yes – surely it is a Soho somewhere, where we passed our youth – guys selling strass from barrows, whispering of horses. Females that trade themselves, or promise to.

'You see,' says Finch, 'It's the whole range – titillation, bit of artistic stripping, little theatres, clubs. Lettuces too, and mangoes here. And in the buildings,' and he pushes my head down to the painted roadway, 'are waiting guys who I, we, never knew. They wait their cue – the famous ones, in photos, ready to come flitting through our lives. Leaders, groups, bands,' and he laughs loud.

The figurines are roughly made, but there's a tiny stamp of life, of difference. If you don't recognise them, it's because you forget the original.

*

In walks the cat. I say, 'It has a most mature gaze.'

Finch says, 'Don't be so solemn about it all. No one keeps a record. It's a cat, just don't exaggerate to make a talking point.'

I say, 'We have to throw ourselves in – this soup of life. Like laying down a fiche, staking, spinning the wheel. It absolves you – everyone is in the game, accepts whatever. Whatever turns up. Like the cat.'

*

'You need a cause,' Finch says, sternly, 'The game can last forever.'

Finch is an awkward guy. My host. He's important too – his name, his family's important, it passes to him, gives him a substance.

There's uprising in the air – even here, rebellion. All this sand.

I scan his books – there's *All You Need to Know about Shrapnel* and *Burns* – not poetry, I guess.

There is a lot of silence. He says, 'Maybe we should try some shooting. I get good stuff, arms and the rest, quite locally – the market.'

I say, 'No, not animals. And are there any here?'

He says, 'No, there's no animals. There's people. That tree's the frontier – just go beyond it, when the bad guys come in trucks ... We shoo them off. They can't pursue – this here's another country.'

'It seems arbitrary,' I say.

'All wars are like this now. The killing, the real stuff, the quantity, it's done in other ways – by famine, the price of pills and rugs ... Then, there's prisons. And the sea. Back you go – the horsemen of the old apocalypse. But here, it's all attrition – big bangs and bombs is out. It's arrangements between the soldieries here, the risk is slight, and none at all for us. Or hardly so.'

I ask, ‘You’re sure the bad guys are authentic, evil?’

He says, ‘Absolutely so. And then – it’s back to eat. I hope you like my pickles. Even if you don’t, that’s what there is.’

He’s shouting now – ‘The rims! The rims, you fool. If you don’t watch it, they jam it up, those bullets jam your gun.’

I say, ‘Of course, I know all that, the loading magazines. It’s just another rule, it’s reason coming through. The guys here – they’ve got computers. They could reason, but they’ve got machines instead. Though it is true, that when the big wave comes, they say it is the Elephant, come to bathe.’

‘Just owning things, even computers, doesn’t make you rational,’ he says. ‘Besides, you must believe in something. If you don’t anthropomorphise bad things, the universe is just a box of curios. It’s not just you, that you’re finite – it’s life, unpleasant all the time. Things need a cause – and so do you. A big thing needs its Elephant.’

He waves his gun. Now, mine’s prepared. He says,

‘I give you just one magazine – even if you load it right, you get to shoot one guy thirty times or so.’

I’m not convinced. I say, ‘You are the strategist, not me.’

He says, ‘We put sheepskins on our heads, so’s not to stick out. It’s not a thing that I do well, this finalising, aiming. Lucky for them that they’re bad guys and we’re bad shots.’

I say, 'I remember, last time I visited, there were lush houses here, not shacks like this. The people came for safety, now they've fled again. Brought it with them, anxiety and peril.'

It had everything, this place. Bars, massages. Just to visit.

Finch says, 'The big change. Revolution. Coming to take repression off our backs.'

He says, 'Even if you get to choose your olive enemy, you won't know his circumstance.'

*

The truck drives by. We shoot. It stops – and here the bad guys come!

I say, 'In the movie, we die.'

Finch says, 'Into that shack – quick, and out the back. No movie.'

I say, 'Wow! An egg. It's quite enormous, on a stand, the mounts look ormolu ...'

'Leave that egg,' he says: 'Don't loot. And drop your weapon too.'

Whatever kind of bird or beast – a roc, a dinosaur – the only thing of interest here, of value. Poor people, just their egg, a conversation piece.

We run. It's not betrayal. I say, 'We could resist some more. More sacrifice.'

'Go ahead!' says Finch.

I wish – that egg. I could have stolen it. And then – tree in the yard, red waxy flowers, they last forever with a little care. The right wall. Right sun. Right family, lots of eyes that watch.

'Yes,' he says, 'You could have tried a cutting. Forget the family bit.'

*

The bad guys move away. Back in their truck. All safe.

Finch carries on: 'The good guys want democracy – each counting fully for himself. Or herself – maybe more complicated, that.'

I say, 'If it's about ones, and being one – they should do everything by themselves, one by one.'

'That's not possible,' Finch says. 'Besides, that leaves you out, nothing for you to do.'

'I am your guest. Then, there's the flags, the pride, the dignity.'

'Pictures! You here for pictures?'

I say, 'Finch, don't be an uncle – every question, every doubt, you put the stopper in the bottle, cork the discourse up. Let things stand outside and open in the sun and oxidise.'

He's offended. He says, 'Don't be embarrassed – everybody runs. That's strategy, and tactics too. We could even catch a train – they must be running still. You need to find a station where they stop. Out here, they go too fast, you can't jump on.'

He's laughing at me now, but he too is scared the bad guys, soldiers, come to look for us. He says, 'I'm well considered here. Some politics, some leadership – being dead, it doesn't do, if you've ambitions.'

*

Back in his house. We, the model memory, we're still in place, his friends, glued down.

He plays a record, says, 'Those old operas – all the sentiments are there, victory, pride, defeat, disappointment. Dignity. Good deaths – well merited. Some vindicated. All by castrati, at that time.'

I say, 'No talk of freedom, of good guys? All that?'

'There is a glimpse, of course. They weren't Neanderthals. Craftsmen, counts, and whores. Mind you, in adolescence, being a castrato's a good deal. I'm quite wistful – you gain years, intrigue in peace, and skip that drizzly time of yearn and loss. Then, back to rutting, with the rest.'

I say, 'All hard to arrange.'

He says, 'Don't be so fucking judicious.'

We sit and face each other. 'Well, what's the moral?' he asks, shoots out his legs, long boots.

We lie, and wait. The bad guys' truck. To take our shot.

Finch is a tiny, mouthy guy. He says, 'If you don't have a cause, you don't become responsible.'

I say, 'Responsible for everything? For all you do? For everyone? Who you do it to? The bad guys in the truck – they're not even our bad guys. I refer, of course, to local bad ones. And besides, there is a pretext always – maybe I mean a context – interests around there are. People – being forced, constrained to do ... what it is they do, what you do.'

He asks, ruffled, 'What you do? What you really do? Or what you intend to do, and what you hope transpires? Intention – before, after, during – what? your mission? Your impulsion?'

We're back to youthful days and arguments. I say – I half recall how it is done, the arguing – 'I mean – free will. Or do I mean free choice? How you put these things – it cuts and wraps up your intent in quite some other ways.'

'That's so much better,' Finch says, 'Leave will out, it's quite too coloured. Let's say you'll shoot because you're motivated. Forget the mechanics of it, free this, free that – or not.'

I say, 'So, being bad guys – you don't think that's part of it? Let's go back, and see what we're responsible for – a sentiment, I guess it is – responsibility, feeling easy with yourself. Suppose you've shot your guy his thirty times ...'

He says, 'You've surely done the thing, but after all, the guy had staked his chip like you. He lets you out. Reciprocity. Don't give it another thought. And there's no law can make you virginal again – though your conscience can!'

We're sweating now. The sun is overhead. He says, irritated,

'If you can pass the time like this, with doubts, maybe you shouldn't be here after all.'

'But I'm your friend, your guest,' I say.

There is a pause. I say, 'You mean, the moment of the act is not the place you think of "why?" or consequence. Give battle, and that's it?'

'In the end, yes. I can't resist, they move me, spur me on, our guys, the good ones. They're so much brighter than the bad. Freedom! Loyalty too, of course. Procedure. Not some big random boss-god, with elephant goad and thunderbolt. Abstractions, rhetoric – that's what draws us in and keeps us going all our lives. A bunch of guys, all waving flags, and shouting 'freedom' – who's not stirred? They say they aren't afraid, they don't fear death. They are unique. Soft lad like you, you want to open doors, breathe in the rose-scent in the garden ... They want to scale the wall and throw it down.'

We sweat some more. I say, 'Those guys and their "free". You say, "I feel free", quite casual, but "I'm free" has quite a different weight, and more specific too. Did Neanderthals say, "I feel free"? Could we expect that of them?'

He fidgets, says, 'No! Not your Neanderthals again – even if they lived round here.'

'Bred in our families. Maybe it's an evolutionary thing. Brains,' I say.

He says, 'Talking of times past – now, you shoot guys the wrong colour, you're in quite another movie.'

'Yes,' I say, 'I should take care. Like shoots on like, guys like me, a tasteful olive colour, we choose the similar. Though olives are mostly green.'

'That fits you, at this moment,' he says.

I say, 'You need a colour chart. Fear's a thing, it turns you green. We're all afraid.'

I say, 'I want to chum along with you, seeing it's your pickles that we're eating. I hadn't thought of taking sides. I'd no intention. Just a holiday, all switched off, or on idle.'

'Hmmmm,' he says. 'Being a guest that's just dropped in – doesn't exclude free choice, free will. It brings it out! The thing's a mystery. Guys here – not the tourists, the real guys – they don't have this gap, hiatus, between their will and action. Their lives – they're like knitted sleeves. They don't drop in on me, unless they're family.'

I say, 'I'm at a loss.'

'If you get your history wrong, some cousin's killed. There's all his family – they're on you all your life. And theirs. Responsibility – the other side of loyalty. You choose your banker wrong – and there's a guy, he's lost his job. He blames you, but it isn't him who pays. You do. It's reasoned out and knitted close, relations here. Cause, will, effect. That's why they have a book that sets the rules. There's just one book, that binds it up – the risk, responsibility – the things you've lost.'

I say, 'Well – mislaid. Got wrong.'

'Exactly. Got them wrong. It's like – you're on a winning cycle, and you can't get off. The same with losing – you must persevere until you win – or can't lose any more. On you go till you fall off, win till you lose. Insanity to stop and interrupt your luck. Luck nothing! It's blind chance, but cyclical.'

If you're in luck, you win until you lose it all. No rest, no pause.

The disc, it plays, and sings, '*cinto ho il crin d'alloro*' – 'my brow is bound with laurel'. We've won, we're safe, the soldiers don't come after us.

*

We spend the evening in a bar.

One of the backing group – she wears a short red dress – makes me see deeper into life than I have ever looked, have ever peered, before. I say,

'My, you're beautiful. Your skin.'

She's been bored out and filled with precious electricity. I say,

'You're Vietnamese?'

'No, I'm American.'

'I mean that too, of course.'

What might I become, being close to her. Even if she went around the world and sang, the being close would be enough – carrying gear, giving her lots of money.

'You're turning to stone,' says Finch.

Now I understand – conversion, afflatus, the stars come down, it runs through you, with no syringe, just through the eyes as if benign juice was flowing in, has hooked you up. This is the spirit, the form you worship, terrible indifferent thing. She says,

'I must go now. It's been pleasant.

'Yes.'

It won't finish, ever.

'You're rather naïve,' says Finch, my friend. Reluctant host.

'That's the first time the truck has stopped,' he says. 'And, if you don't mind, don't mention the sheep, the skins.'

I say, 'I can't imagine why you settle for your people here, boosting you up. Power – hmmm. Why don't you choose freedom. Some kind of it. You know it isn't in the state. Nor praying. Poetry. All those vain things.'

'Settle for it?' he asks, 'It's here, on hand. Of course, I'd have liked something – other. All my own. Who wouldn't? Let's get rid of the oppressor here, maybe the one over there, beyond the tree, the bad guys ... the real bad guys ... But – I still value you, old friend, and all the others. Old friends.'

'What's that to do with anything?' I ask.

## Dea

Home again. Here's Dea, wearing her bright clothes and smile. Full of joy. She says, 'It seems friend Finch's well thought of, by the highest,' and I say,

'He invited me to some shooting. People.'

'He's always been tough on the bad guys. Did you hit something?'

'A truck, I think. Lots of poor people around. Sand, not much else. Oppression, though it was out of sight.'

'Finch isn't in finance,' she says. 'Poverty is not a remit. He's powerful now, and it's growing. He doesn't forget his friends.'

'He lives poorly – that's his plan. He models us. We're in this tiny Soho. He remembers me – outside a peepshow.'

I don't tell her – the backing group. My love. Is it best – searching for ever for what's lost? Finding at the last? Or just following – a trail, the posters. Gig on mega-gig. Careers and fortunes, up and down, not a hunt – a follow, never finding.

I say, 'Yes, we're all there, glued down, in remembered postures.'

'He was always a formalist,' says Dea. 'Odd in other ways. We were once about to do some sex, but his religion came in.'

'He was always twitchy about contacts,' I say. 'That's why he glues us down – to stop us gliding away.'

'He has this "great man" thing,' she says. 'Wants to steer the galleys. Better than rowing, that's for sure. He lets his family do that.'

'There you were, Dea, old friend, minute, on Finch's roadway. Across the street from me, my figure, homuncule. Cakes or hats? – you're peering in a window, I can't make it out, how he remembers you. Are you a hat person? Surely not,' I say.

'No.'

'Then it was a patisserie. Then there's Luca, optimistic and alone, face half-upturned, upward if never onward, in the window whore or siren, behind the curtain there.'

'Why'd Finch choose that street?' she asks. 'Memory laid out like a train set, or a porcelain orchestra. All of us?'

'It's where we all criss-crossed. There was a consulate, wholesale jewels, butchers' knives – that insurrectionary bookshop. We were all committed then, the street both lofty and banal – was made for us. High intensity, and full indifference.'

'It's Proust in plasticine,' she says. 'Finch and his tiny visions.'

I say, 'It's where I found my quest – the Path, the Light. That's quite an enterprise.'

'Meanwhile,' she says, 'you yaw about in all directions.'

'Those guys who do the books,' I say heavily, 'sitting in rooms, or in deckchairs – they talk of realms ... of freedom, justice, all that stuff, of how they make a space, a mountain top, there you feel free ... Read, listen, drink it all down. Better than fighting, sex, or states, all that. Then there's us guys, the rest – we want to act, to do the things. "The Tenth Red Army went to meet its end." Now, that is real, it makes you want to do, to stir,' and I go on.

She says, 'You're making me laugh.'

I say, to finish, 'Long sentences,' and turn away.

We must find the path – a way to live our lives their good, best way. And stir things too. Dea says, 'You – shooting guys – it's just the opposite of what we were ... It makes me sad, when living is so tough.'

Now Odile's with us, and she says the trouble is, we have no cash. 'My idea is,' she says, 'The people love religious stuff, the martyrs, suicides, all that. They say they don't, can't understand, but look! You do a try-out on some epic movie set. You do a stunt. You throw yourself, down from some tower. You land quite bad, and break yourself. But it's insured, and so you leave with heaps of cash.'

Odile – she smiles, that innocent stupid face, I'd throw myself for you, I say, and she says,

'Well, you had your chance with me, you blew it, and besides, you're not a victim, you're too mean, beneath your innocent, your stupid air.'

I say to Dea, 'This idea – a kind of accidental suicide. Not quite insurance fraud – the hurt is real, it's the intent...'

Dea says, ‘That’s crap. This area’s quite rich, even for guys like us that think they don’t fit in – we hang around the table, stuff to eat falls off, for sure. The banqueting goes on, until it all goes bad, then maybe lots of other guys come bustling in. More deserving.’

I’m irritated – ‘What’s deserving to do with it? What do we deserve? Maybe those others won’t come in, they’ll stay put on their atlas page and just have fun – those guys that throw the water paint or stage the fights with animals – why would they leave their good time, come and grey-out here, this tilt and slide, apocalypses like a rash – your knees and elbows all afire with short-time working, documents adrift, all that.’

*

Mansour the destitute – he says, ‘I’m a martyr to spectacle.’ He has become an infant, in a basket, all broken up and disconnected. Took Odile’s advice, and jumped. He says,

‘I don’t suppose God knows about insurance fraud, or me. Insurance you can see as insult to Him, that’s why He talks in generalities, like preachers in the street.’

‘You pried,’ I tell him, ‘Looked into the machine and saw the wheels that turn. You’re not supposed to do that – accidents should stay as such. God doesn’t look at mechanisms, only actions. Yours was decisive – stupid too.’

Dear old friend. What a mess. A fraud gone wrong – he's smashed himself to get the cash that pays for him to lie here, smashed.

He says, 'My mind is better than it's ever been.' But no, it's tangled with his body, his ambition, the cash to do quite other things, a talk with God, maybe, when both had time to spare.

I say, 'Mansour, it isn't you – you're just the picture of an error, what it isn't worth to do.'

*

Odile says, 'Finch? You've been with Finch, that reedy little chap, all blobs and spots? Who said I was his girl. Makes models of us all, his friends? How do I look?'

'There's a figure on the sidewalk, bent over and in tears.'

'Then it's not me,' she says. 'I remember – we had a kind of sex one time. But it was you was interested in me, or so I thought.'

I say, 'It's not the sex we want, and not the hunt, the conquest, as it's called. It's culture – all the coloured tasty things that women waft around.'

'You're gay,' Odile says.

I say, 'Don't let's start into that. It's just my civilisation, wants to trample into yours.'

'You missed your chance,' she says, 'By fifty years or more.'

*

'What a prude you are,' says Dea, 'Saving up your life – what do you expect to spend it on? That time?'

She shouts at me, and grips the muscle in my arm, and there's her thigh, pressed against mine –

'And now, you try to tell me what I know, what I believe, is stupid, superficial.'

I say, 'But no ...'

'You're just like Finch, you throw a stone – some guy's beliefs, their thoughts, all smashed and holed. My temple, group, my party – all the rituals – not worth your time, the time you've so much of because you never spend the fucking stuff, you store it up and maybe throw it in the sea when I don't look and check on you. I'd have gone and shot those bastards if they asked me, killed them if that's what you have to do – and no one brings them back or asks you why, no one complains – or if they do, they don't know who you are. And they don't care. Sometimes that truck, the one you shot, will stop: the guys come after you – you run, that's what your little legs are for. Sometimes you hit the truck, sometimes you hit a guy, because Finch took you there and in his tiny head he's calculated all the chance, that they won't stop. And gets it wrong. You've calculated too, all day. You get it right. The truck will stop. And you are scared. You're right, and Finch is wrong. So, it's all the same, and both of you just little birds that's shaken out their tree ...'

'Rest!' I say, 'Hold your peace.'

'No! Test first,' says Dea. 'Time to climb the tree,' and here's some sticky pads with nails. And here's the tree. She fastens on her pads, and now she's halfway up – a thirty metre palm. I'm still here, on the ground.

'No, not on your feet, those pads,' she shouts, 'You're not an ape. The pads on hands and knees,' and up I go. We're squirrels, and she says, 'The hard part's going down headfirst: those animals – if they can manage, so can we.'

We're at the top, and here's a nest. Our bodies arched – we should be face to face, but in between there is the trunk. And here's the eggs – 'No, no,' I shout, but she has cast them down, the mother bird's aghast, and down they go – but as they fall, they hatch, and out fly parakeets, like darts of red and blue. They already have their songs and trill around, their memory is full at birth, their life is halfway done before it starts.

'You see?' she shouts, 'You have your memory filled with how to climb – except those pads are not provided in the womb ...'

I ask, 'The hatch?'

She says, 'There is a scientific reason, which I now forget. We force them to be free. But – we expect no thanks.'

*

That second day with Finch. He thinks those soldiers may come back. We never see the cat again – maybe it's wise, or lost

I say, 'Your street, with all of us – will it seem magic, if the soldiers come, and will they let it be? Or think the magic's black, and burn it up?'

He says, irritated, 'Those guys aren't into voodoo. Best, though, we both go off a day or two.'

He climbs up on his horse, and pulls me up behind. He says, 'The horse will always come in first, he always wins, though only by a neck. He suffers more. And you,' he shouts, as we trot on, 'Are always last.'

In town, he has an office. Clients, penitents, and supplicants around. He says,

'This town has lots of beggars now – bad sign. The thieves reduced to begging – means hard times. These guys – they come to ask, for sure, but also tell. I'm fishing in them. If not truth, intelligence.'

He blesses them, and waves his hands. He says – a ritual – 'God is great. Come back Thursday.' I say,

'Thursday's today.'

He says, 'That's quite what I am saying,' and all round there is a mumbling, threats, and stories longer than your memory, solutions beyond your prayers, vendications that would scare you, and I say,

'The group, performing in that bar – there was a girl that stood and sang, part of the band. I didn't catch her name, nor where they'd go ...'

He says, offhand, 'They went to Africa: a little place, you'll not get there by bus. A place called Yebbi, Chad, think, you'd need to ask. But in a year or two they'll all be back, and full of song.'

*

'As cheeses go,' says Finch, 'I'm pretty big – but they don't have cheeses here. The third day: that's the big one of your stay. The last. And forget that short red dress – it takes you through the world, all over; you won't remember what you see. She is no help. Not a small bit.'

*

I tell Dea about the second day. The petitioners. God is great. Come back Thursday.

*

That tree – better than sex, more mystery too.

Then, later, Odile says, 'You know, that Dea's dead.'

I hadn't heard. I say, 'I know.'

'You didn't visit. That's exactly like you,' says Odile, and she's exactly right. She says,

'Dea had a kind of ecstasy. Living too much. Exploded. And she died.'

'Gone, you mean?'

Odile says, 'No, of course, she's still here, it's just she doesn't speak or listen.'

'Well,' I say, 'That's not so bad, then.'

We find a doctor, and he says, 'Ah, Dea, yes. We made an egg around her.'

So they did. She lies there, a huge egg, unadorned, quite shiny, it shimmers in the sun, and when they light the candles round her bed at night, it glows.

'She didn't lay the egg herself, of course,' the doctor says – 'that would be paradox, and absurd. To make one's habitat, lie there, still, and well – a bit complacent, don't you think? Of course, it's nourishment, though how she uses it is, well ...'

Odile says, 'You don't seem to know a lot about it,' and he says,

'The moment of the birth, the hatching – that is what we wait and pray for. Birth and cure. The revelation. What's been taken in, assimilated. Where she's been. Gone down, flown up ...'

'You mean, she may have wings?' asks Odile, surprised, and I think of the parakeets which flew away like darts. And Finch, the little pecking man, all blotched and fluting, his nickname fitting, flitting all round him. 'Yes, well,' says Odile, 'Quite like an egg it is.'

The doctor is quite irritated, 'We call it "egg", it's our invention, if you like, a metaphor. Don't get sucked in by literalness. Stick to realism – that's best. And Dea – when they brought her in, she was the colour of cigars, that comes to those who sleep out doors, and cook their food in oildrums ...'

'The bill. We pay when she hatches,' says Odile.

'That could be difficult,' I say, 'and women should enfold – forget the shaman stuff. This egg business, can go on forever, like the costs.'

'That's life,' says Odile, not much interested. 'And Mansour – his choice, and not my fault.'

'Life, life!' I say. 'Is that your mantra?'

'This egg therapy,' she says, 'it's standard.'

*

It's the third day. Finch and I – we both sleep on Finch's desk.

'The trouble with my memory house,' he says, 'Is that it's not just me that changes, it is you, my friends. The leader of our cell, that Luca – now, he's depressive. And you've grown out of sex, the peepshows too. Who knows what next?

'And now I must pursue some guys – it's not like you, that hunting of the girl, the one that couldn't sing too well. The hunt is universal – there's always guys that's after you, as soon as you move up in life. That actor guy – he put it well. He was a celebrated ham – the actor in this play. Then, he becomes the hamlet in his playlet! Wrote it, as if he wasn't really there in dreamland – but the nub is clear. They sent out guys to kill him! Families! And now I find myself besieged – there's always bombers, ministers and priests – they stop you doing what you know is right ...' and on he goes.

We hunt his guys, his killers – down in the tunnelled city, hard to say if we are underground or not – there is no ground, the passages are on the roofs of hovels down below, and those in turn ... It looks the same all over: there is that little girl with wistful look, a pile of awful stuff, a dog a-rolling up his eyes, over and over, round and round. Ah yes, the tedium ...

'Mind, mind out! – a well! right in the middle of the path! This place – it all needs tearing down, but then they'll build it up again,' says Finch. 'Those guys, I think there's two of them. One does the deed, the other checks on him. Or maybe her – we mustn't live by stereotype.' I ask,

'And if we find them?'

'We confront them! They should be ashamed.'

It doesn't seem decisive, and I say, 'As you move up and into fame, there'll always be these guys or similar, so why ...?'

'That's true, so true,' he says. 'That's life. Remember – that game was prettied up for kids: they put some ladders in, where here was only snakes. For here, in life, there's only snakes, and wells concealed, and in your way.'

We travel on, the city never ends, or we are in another city, so it seems – and is the soldiery at work, and do they trash the memory, the figures in the shack ...?

The killers – we don't find them. 'Well, that's sport,' says Finch, quite satisfied: 'I hope your holiday's been fun – you leave this afternoon. Bear my tidings where you came from, to all the other dear old friends.' And so it goes.

## Luca

When we were young and free, Luca led our little group, he did what gurus do, instructed: then we split.

In the archive, Luca is consolidating.

I'm with Odile. He says, 'Mind, Odile, – you too. Traitors both.' Lots of paper stuff around.

'We're here because you are our optimist,' I say.

These are state archives, he's made piles of boxes, and I see – M for massacres, T for torture. Then, there's C for complicity – perhaps the tallest pile. He moves some documents around. He says,

'With this, I've nailed them – PB for promises not maintained, CO for covert ops.'

'Shouldn't it be dates and people?' asks Odile.

'What difference does it make?' he asks. His glance is sour. I say,

'Aren't you too moralistic with all this stuff? For after all, it's life, is how things are, you could discriminate...' and he leaps in, 'Yes, D: discriminat-ion. That's in the other room.'

'An archive is itself a judgement,' Luca says. 'You should see the stuff I've thrown away.'

I think of shooting at the truck with Finch, and say, 'It looks like morals have the upper hand,' and he is angry, and he says,

'The categories – look at them. They're quite descriptive. I don't prescribe a thing,' and he stuffs some photos in another box.

'What's you two parasites up to now?' he asks. Odile replies,

'There's a crew, a gang – I do some culture with them – dance, gymnastics, painting with our bodies. Keeps us on the street,' and Luca says, 'You don't need apologise. It's just – I have a proper job. Memory – I'm its keeper, as you see,' and that is true.

Odile – she picks at her rough clothes, each day she takes them from a box.

'And you?' Luca asks, grudgingly. I say,

'Oh well, I'm in between things. Finch is going fierce. I visit there.'

'Your grand inaction!' he says, 'And Finch takes up the family trade. There's things are bubbling there, but I fear – the socialism we used to mention, that will only come with penury. When there's nothing left to eat, and we are fried – it's then we'll start to share.'

We stare at each other. Then,

'I'll take you to the square,' he says, 'There's some real people there. My guys.'

The bar is called the Paradise, some guys are doing bets.

'They just look ordinary criminals,' Odile says, 'Like in every square.'

'Yes, that is so,' says Luca, 'But they're soft and stupid underneath – they can be turned, they're my Red Wedge, and when the time comes round, they'll be my vanguard.'

Odile says, 'They don't look soft to me. I think it's good that you have kept some optimism, though.'

There's nowhere for us two to go. We don't much like each other, Odile and I.

We go to Finch.

He says, 'So! Dea is an egg – she may be hatched as Venus. Or as Spring. A lizard, or an albatross. And Mansour! In his basket! Like the guy, dismembered in the rope trick, can't be put together, stuffed in some file in Luca's fancy,' and he laughs. I say,

'That Soho street – you need redo it all.'

'Finch says you could build a hotel here,' Odile says. We stare out across the dunes. I say,

'Yes, you could.'

That song says, 'Get out of the new land.' Times change.

I say, 'We can't afford these new prices.'

She says, 'You could get a job like Luca,' and I say,

'No, I couldn't.'

No thought comes into our head, and then I say,

'Your mouth tastes of walnuts.'

'Yes,' she says, 'That's rather good.'

This place here – it must have been a burial ground – most places are. A civilisation moves away, maybe left some genes, but not the language, not an architecture, no wood for cooking, no stones ...

'Look, look!' says Odile. 'The ghosts, the ghosts – you need some ghosts to give a place like this some life,' and maybe we can see them, wreathing round, the dance that lasts for days, and carries you from season's end to marriage, a new cycle of divinities – one special god that looks at you all sour, he blights – and so – on, on to Sacrifice! Oh no, that lovely lady goat ... and Odile says,

'A swimming pool quite breaks the spell.'

*

'I suppose I'm Finch's girl,' she says.

I say, 'My girl's on tour. I recognise the group, but not her name.'

She says, 'That kind of music often doesn't come again.'

'Those tours – they go around the world. Who knows what will be transformed. Art!' I say, and laugh.

*

People marching down the road. Green flags, red flags.

The revolution! – we've been waiting for, since we were young and sang the songs – the change no one foresaw, but we've expected, all our lives. So, here it is: it's no surprise. The risks ...

'Where do we stand?' asks Odile, 'With Finch? These guys want each to count for one – and no more torture. We're his guests – what if these guys go after him? Is there exemption, some protocol, an etiquette, for friends, for guests?' I say,

'He said to come back Thursday – that's today. Maybe he planned it all. Or else it's office hours.'

She says, 'The big guys – when the people move their feet, they always look for terrorists.'

I say, 'Maybe, Odile, you are a suspect? Your street group. Performance? Makes you a target,' and she laughs.

'Finch, does he steal?' I ask.

'He doesn't do finance,' she says, 'He's never lent me, though I've asked.'

*

'Some guys here, want things to go back like they never were, and start their lives and do it right this time,' I say. 'And other guys just want to start.'

'Now,' says Finch, 'People won't come to ask for things, they'll tell me what they want. They will be heavier.'

'More frustrated,' says Odile.

'We'll suffer more,' I say. 'Knowing what we want and all the reasons why we can't.'

'Does Luca still have guys ... that bar? The Paradise?' asks Finch. 'He has the big change in his mind. It's coming here, of course, but people want such different things.'

I think: – one of those things – on tour in Chad.

'It's easy to be trivial,' says Odile. 'And it keeps you safe.'

Finch says, 'I'll have to change the model now, if it's survived. Luca's pure flame. We can't forget him. Now too, there's Dea in her egg, poor Mansour ...'

'I may stay here, now revolution's come,' I say, 'and find myself a role.'

Finch stares. 'Here, take this cash,' he says, and gives us suitcases. They're full: 'You pass through bad guys' land – just over there, beyond those trees. The buses there still run. And when you're home, you put it in the bank...' and here is the address.

'I may be president,' he says, 'Or maybe not.'

*

When we're alone, I ask Odile, 'Is this the stolen cash?'

She says, 'We could just find a place, under a floor, and leave it till we see what's what. Or use it for expenses – there'll be lots.'

'I'd rather give it to some real revolutionaries,' I say.

'Those are the first to end up in the jail, or at the wall,' she says.

‘Finch loves and trusts us, that’s for sure,’ I say, ‘That room, the figurines ...’

‘You can’t be sentimental when it comes to moving on,’ she says, vaguely. I think – her mouth, her hands. I say,

‘It’s not exactly moving on, from here, from Finch – it’s just, politically ...’

‘Exactly,’ says Odile, and off we go.

In bad guys’ land, it’s true, the buses run.

Guys steal the cash, and that resolves the deal, it seems.

I say, ‘We should have asked them for receipts. To show we’re in good faith. But, after all, Finch trusts us and he loves us – so he won’t suspect ...’

‘And if he did, he would be wrong,’ she says: ‘In revolutions, love is rarely on the order of the day. As Engels said ...’

But we both know what Engels said, for that is part of youthful days, and now we have to leave the bad guys’ land, somehow, and find a nest for one, or two, and then I say,

‘Oh no – if things go bad for Finch, he’ll come and stay ...’ and Odile says that friendship has its limits, everyone knows that, and all we had from him was running and escaping, pickle sandwiches, and rhetoric. That is all.

The land is orderly, so no one thinks to help us, destitutes. But there are always guys who’re after us, they follow, they suspect.

We walk along, we look around. Then, Odile says,

'Now, you must jump off this cliff. With me, and trust me.'

'Why?' I ask.

'Because it's love. It's life. Besides, there's bad guys after us – you see them running. What can they want? We've nothing left – so, it's the priceless things, the things you'd never think to sell, they're after.'

I think of Dea in her shell, and Mansour, basketed – I envy them, they're safe, suspended. Yet there's Odile – maybe you need that other body, when it feels at rest, and tired, and needs you ... Into my head comes poetry about the years, of 'blur and blot', and when you think of need, what need is that? An airy way of saying 'want', and ...

Now she takes me by the hand – the bad guys are upon us, and she pulls, she jumps, and I fall after.

It is a classic fall, like Icarus with a passenger, Eve who betrays her Adam, leads him to her softer garden, warm cuddling in the grass – snakes all around, with agate eyes.

We fall, we drop, for years, it's slow, didactic, and we twist, we gyre. The cliff is like a home for bees. Here there are cells – a guy is leaning here, chin on the window ledge, at rest, at peace: beside him there's his dog, a collie, with no sheep to set in clumps. They're clearly in for life, and on the next floor down – my! they're torturing and looking grim. The guys, the torturers, are pondering – the right test, question, for their quest. You overstress – you kill the tortured guy, he's gone, indifferent, maybe, or ignorant. The four last words – 'what do you know', 'what have you learned'...

It makes you think of God or judgement, when they ask, 'What did you make of it, the galaxies with different clocks, the stars too black to see or shine, the infinitely small that you don't know exists, the infinitely large that you've no way to measure. Well, what do you make of it? Does it make sense to you?' Or if it does to someone else, what does it signify? – 'you understand'? What? And on it goes, the torture, judgement, punishment on punishment, you – ignorant, you impotent, and 'yes' you cry, 'yes, yes, I understand, I'm bottom of my class, I see the wonders, marvellous they are, some cretin must have spent a million years to think it up, this great complexity, when all I want – is someone's mouth that tastes of something ... Maybe a job, – no weekend working, please.'

'Come on, come on!' It's Odile, 'Hurry on, down, down, and we'll be safe.'

I say, 'We're safe already – off the cliff, and as we fall, we're out of reach. And when we hit the bottom, well – they always say "you can't fall any further", and you start again ...'

She says, she weeps, 'No, no. We hit, and then – well, I don't want to start again. Not you I want – but just a steady state – with maybe you,' though that's not what I have in mind – and down we go, the simple thing is not so easy now, and here's a scene – some boss and guys all sitting round. There's ones who run the upper storeys, and far down, far, far below, the cuirassiers who stand on guard. This is the whole, the state. And round about, the huts, with thatch – I think, maybe we'll hit a hut, but iron roofs have come in as well, there's not much hope for us. And Odile says,

'You're so naive, this stuff about the state and bad guys, prison and torture, sure we need the law, and lockups, lockdowns, what the hell you please – you just avoid to hit the floor, but all the bad guys ask us for is meaning, values, all that stuff. They know that what we are will make us scream, cry out. And tell – whatever comes into our head. It's speech they want, communication. They don't want secrets. Just to hear your voice, say what they want, wring out the words, you've given in to them ... they hear you speak, and know – that what we are is pain, annihilation. That's the lesson,' and we fall, fall on and on, and on she goes.

'Odile, that's terrible,' I say. 'In these few hours of fall – I see that all your life is full of dark and doubt ...'

And then we're down. We scamper off, two innocents – we didn't eat the fruit or anything, in that rich peaceful land, that hid its evil fairly well. Who'd trust a stranger anyway, with fruit, who offered you the truth? We drifted down – the poems, colours, tags and haikus, all flow through your mind, and then! You're down.

'We'll catch our boat, or bus,' she says. 'We're immigrants.' And so we are – we come, we go, we answer all the while, express our hopes and fears, duress or not – some lies, to all the bad guys there who ask.

Sometimes we say we know friend Finch, and other times we don't.

I say, 'Finch loved us, in the end,' and Odile says, 'That teaches us,' but what, she doesn't say.

Finch. We never tell him that his money's gone. He never asks. He trusts us and he loves us, maybe he models us again. He doesn't trace us, maybe he doesn't try. We're just two figures, running on his floor, like other figurines.

Odile and I – we've nothing, and we cling, we fall into each other, like they say, and we're gone, we're lost. She takes me, leads me – through the dark, her dark, the underground, the night. Bodies don't speak, don't mean, they have no quest, nowhere to go, no ending, happy, unhappy. They just stop. Nothing.

'Odile, you're dark,' I say. I mean, she has no light.

She says,

'Yes, that is so. And you – you're air and empty, just a waft.'

*

Luca's working on the C's. 'I want to keep them separate,' he says: 'Corruption – that's a heap. Then Cataclysm – must leave more space for that. Then Capitalism ...' and he fusses up and down.

I say, 'You soldier on, dear Luca, but your troops – where have they gone?'

'I've found another lot,' he says, 'Not just shock troopers in the bar. The young guys hate the octopus as well. It's just they haven't got the analytic gaze, the theoretic turn ...'

'The news of Finch ...' I start to say.

'Finch – borne from the scaffold to the desk!' he says, 'Now Minister of War. And all the family too, all cared for,' and I say,

'He loves me, but he doesn't care for me. I guess that leaves me clean.'

'You want some cash?' asks Luca: 'Join with Odile, gymnastics in the square. The cultural lilt and sway – denounce the bad guys with a tune: it does no harm, it keeps you fit ...' He doesn't say 'fit for the big day', but it's there, there in his heart.

'It's not the dance, you fool,' Odile shouts. 'The money's in the booze. We serve the people, when the show is done.'

'The fact is,' Luca says, quite undisturbed, 'that where Finch is, it's true the north and south are democrats. They're what you call the heavy ones, each counts as one, and not as chip or flake of tribe. Or clan, religion, all that stuff. The trouble is, they hate each other. Us here – once we were heavy people too, but now we've gone all light. It happens. Finch now – hmmmm. Still, he's a contact, I suppose,' and he talks on, of solidarity, of big and little states, of revolution, sell-outs, long times. A noble soul – and Odile whispers, 'My! He's all alone.'

I say, 'What you say is easy, Odile,' and she shouts at me,

'You fragment! It's life we need, not Luca shifting alphabets. Move around, King Log! Be a driver, drive a truck! And find another woman!'

Maybe I shall. Not yet. A postcard comes from Chad, it says – 'to my unknown admirer': 'unknown's' crossed out, instead there is 'unnamed'. 'We have a gig where first we met. I'll see you there. There's no concessions, though.'

She's been and sung and left. That short red dress ...

Address – that comes from Finch, no doubt.

*

I say, 'Luca, the movement's circular – of everything – for sure. It's like the guys that walk around the flying mountain peak – that keeps it anchored, keeps you fit, the demon's charmed with flattery. You hope the mountain doesn't fly away, and so you stamp your feet upon its slopes and make your joyful noise – those drums, the cymbals, hear the rams' horns blare – and so you circle round. Mount Hope ...'

Luca says, 'Truth is a certain kind of freedom, though it doesn't work beyond these walls. Odile's – is strass. And yours is – nothing. And surely, Finch will do his best,' dismissively, then, 'Yes, lots of comrades went into mysticism, a continent with many provinces, but all of them look much the same. All with a too-human face. It's just a way of passing time – you pass so much, you think time's gone for good ...'

I say, 'I fear that Luca's right – I'm impatient, though, can't take his discipline,' and Odile sniffs and turns away. Luca concludes,

'If it's emptiness you seek – that's what you'll find for sure.'

'We must go look for those suitcases,' says Odile, 'If we don't find them, full, we'll go see Finch. Remember, I'm his girl.'

I say, 'It sounds like seeking flying mountains: suitcases, empty or full, hard to pin down.'

She objects, 'People look for treasure everywhere, they always have.'

'That's surely true,' I say, 'But you might say our treasure has been found – the guys that stole it, bad fruits all – they were the ones who found.'

'It's so medieval, this kind of argument,' she says. 'It's even got a Latin name, that I forget. It's castrating, your chop and chaff. Let's go, let's go and seek.'

And so we do.

Of course, the badness done in bad guys' land is done invisibly – I mean, we don't see it being done. It's true, the guys are light, they don't talk much, the traffic moves in tidy lines, cops have that smile. It's quite like home.

We find the suitcases. Empty. On sale.

'We must buy them, and show them to Finch,' Odile says.

'I don't think so,' I say. 'The truth's our last resort. It is the most unlikely part.'

This land is clean. I say, 'They take the poor guys' shoes away, they can't go out and spoil the views. If some guy you don't know, comes up and whispers 'things are bad' you know they're bad. In good guys' lands, no one will talk to you, the stranger – they just complain among themselves.'

Odile objects – 'About the shoes – that seems untrue. I hate it when you lie to me.'

I think – suppose Dea doesn't hatch, and Mansour doesn't recompose and climb his rope? And Luca's truth and socialism – what if it stays in those small rooms – what then?

We go to Finch.

Finch says, 'We're seriously at war – the floor below, that Ministry – Defence. My guys may lose. But bad guys' land – it stays the same. They interfere. Those guys are light. We, the newly heavy ones – just now, I can't give what they want. They can't take it either. In the end, it's war or peace.'

There is no talk of cash. I say, 'The Path? You've found the Path?'

'Just now,' says Finch, 'It isn't up to me. There's millions on the watch, some search, and most have given up the quest.'

*

'Guys here,' says Finch, 'they care, they're cared for. Change is a torment, it cuts deep.' He says: 'Do we want to lose all that, tranquillity? Change like the wind – whisks you away, poor things. Ours is a smaller world than yours, but warm, intense. God speaks.'

He pushes us into the corridor: 'That's why you're still my friends, and why I don't ask you for the money. Trust. Loyalty. Courage.'

'Rather summary,' I say, outside. 'I'm not convinced,' and Odile says she's still his girl, perhaps. We leave the building, there is battle there. Outside as well. The guys are running, so's the cops. 'All will be resolved,' she says. We can't resist. We run.

'Not a good time to ask for a loan,' I say.

Later – 'Ah, my good friends! Though much reduced,' says Finch.

Sounds of conflict within, without.

Suddenly he shouts, 'And here you are again! I give you cash. And hospitality. My memories. The story of our youth, the good time – oppressed, intelligent, carefree.'

We know that, we don't want to hear it all again. He says,

'My guys, the good ones, here embattled – I've to find some cops to put the bad ones into jails,' and he's puffed out, quite circular.

Odile says, 'All revolutions go like that, for a while at least,' it's a mistake to speak, he's angry, once again we scuttle down the stairs. We pass some doors, Defence,

Finance – there's guys with guns and counting notes, we're in the street, there's networks being split and rocks are thrown. I say,

'It's a mistake to speak.'

We skirt disputatious crowds. 'This – this uprising should be close to us,' I say, 'Guys on the boil. Close to our core. Why don't we feel it so?'

'It's reason,' Odile says, 'It corrodes us. We keep turning pages, looking at the end – the book is over when it's just begun.'

I say, 'When Petrarch did his poems, crowds gathered in the street, then, wet off the press, the sheets were passed around.'

'That's long ago,' she says.

'It's just a thing you know about,' I say.

I think of Dea.

From inside her egg she says, 'Lift me up – and cast me down.'

The doctors say, 'Oh noooo,' they come and sing to her, she doesn't make a nuisance, not a smell, a blot of something. In my mind, I say,

'Let's take her up the tree, or up the cliff, and throw her down, maybe she'll hatch as she descends, or maybe not – her destiny, it all comes out. Too much intensity. Life broke her, but inside she's white and clean, not like poor Mansour, broken up.'

'It's armies in the end,' says Odile wisely. 'They decide.'

We run from group to group: 'Avoid the Third Force,' says Odile. 'They shoot.'

All have to eat, and so there's grills and such, all improvised, and there we get our food. We are suspected, and when we're carried off for questioning, she says, 'We're spies.' That way we're all content, and there's some truth in what she says.

'We love your cause,' I say, 'but we just want to get away and sort things out.'

*

'That isn't "baby pink", although the bottle says as much, it's really Cadillac, pink like the Fifties automobiles,' and Odile pinks her nails. She has a little telephone, it's ivy-green and cranberry. She's wearing plimsolls, white as swans, black leather jacket, and her hair is streaked as if she's from the bottom of the sea. She's irresistible.

Finch clings, his desk is tilting, crowds shout for his death – or his eternal life. It moves us, this new movement, and its shadow's cast upon our memory – just now, the theme is mostly running.

'Dea so wants to be hatched as something new,' I say, 'and Mansour to be put together.'

'I'm happy I don't want things like that,' Odile says.

'Maybe today's a day Finch wants to see us,' says Odile.

'Aha!' says Finch. 'It's you again – don't want to stay, don't want to go. I know just how you feel. But – all that cash I gave you – where can that have gone? Was all for you.' He wrings his hands.

I say, 'Then there's the other countries, and some guys are fused with bitterness – some for the past, some for the cash they're losing now. And justice too...'

'Yes, justice,' and Finch rocks his desk, and looks around the room.

'Off with his head,' shouts Odile, several times.

'My dear,' says Finch. 'Your colours uncoordinate – quite irresistible. If only I'd the time for you. My operas too – there's executions there, and people riled, love makes you sing a storm – an aria: the word means air, and that is running out. The new is being born, it's gasping – will it suffocate? Or learn to march in step, and win the hour? It's quite a mystery, my friends. I love you both, of course, don't let me down and have me recompose my memory – the room was trashed, of course, the cat, who knows ... but still, the figurines ...' and he shows some lumps, like uncooked dough, unreachable by therapy, crushed up, like poor Mansour. He says,

'Not all will make it to the Path.'

'Yes, yes!' I say, 'that's what I seek. The Path. Maybe illuminated – just a squeak of light, a needle-eye, no more.'

He stares at us, speechless now, bored, suspicious, disillusioned.

Another guy comes in: Finch says, as if it is an interview resumed, 'This revolution—' He's interrupted – 'Uprising', 'Protest,' 'Internet surge ...'

The guy says, 'Suitcases have gone missing. Probably financing guys abroad.'

Finch says, 'I'm sorry for the old guys, as they die so easy. They've invested so many years, protected, loved and squandered – the old ones should go on. The young ones – they know nothing, and they're strong. Let them suffer destinies.'

Odile whispers to me, 'That would let us out. A theft to order isn't theft. We just delivered them, those cases.'

'You must know,' says Finch, 'How I love models. You, my friends, were just a fancy, putty. But now, I've made a space, I've put some ministries together – war, finance, defence. That's freed a vast expanse. Now, I can lay them out, the model citizens.'

'Tell us,' says Odile.

'Each makes a model of themself. They put it near some other guy they feel is close, a network that protects them. That way, still, each counts as one, and no one more than one.'

'It's Toytown,' says Odile.

'Well – yes and no,' he says. 'Of course, it's fun. Guys like to climb up high to see the little towns, and tiny people scurrying. It all goes back to when we lived in trees, and threw nuts down upon our friends. Of course, trees are just a metaphor – as Dea knew, before her joyful accident. The tree of life! The trees that breathe and give us back our air, they're towers that nature gives – and takes away ...' and on he goes. I say,

'Forget the trees, the metaphors. What does this expanse, these figurines – what purpose do they serve?'

He holds his secret close, he pauses long and dry. Then,

'Guys, people – I reckon one in three wants flags. And speeches. Some marching up and down, but not too much. Being told what's what, and there's an end. One in twenty is with Luca, wants new life. The rest – they want their pay, their holidays, their evenings on the porch. Believe in what they like, and don't explain. The marching up and down is only for the festive days, the rest is being left alone.'

'It's flat and inconclusive,' Odile says.

'There is another side, of course,' Finch says. 'The standard model's only putty, but to make a buck for us, for you to climb a rung or two – we have some guys that carve you out in gold, or diamonds too. It costs – but you are something more, you sparkle in the lights, you don't go out of shape when some guy treads on you.'

I say, 'It all sounds bland. A little tired.'

'But wait!' he says. 'There's no one stays there all their life – not even diamond guys. If things go bad, there's hazards there. There is the Gutter – quite explains itself. You end up there, you turn into a primal lump. Then, there is the fiery chariot. It calls for you, you disappear. We scoop you up. To heaven? Going to heaven? Well, you'll have to wait and see. The thing is, once you're gone, you're gone. Being a model citizen is not for ever.'

'A dynamic mode, yes,' says Odile, 'That is what you need.'

'Of course,' says Finch, 'I leave out things – like what is real and what is good, the how, the why. They argued over it for years – it's left me quite dissatisfied. But – real destinies, that's what hits you hard, and even thirty times, bang bang! For after all, if there's no chance, no luck, no fate, no mystery – what is the point? We're better off in trees, and gathering nuts to throw them down. Now, if you see these model guys, tiny but quite representative, some made of precious things, some not, some badged in black, and one in twenty badged in red – you'll see I'm not a cynic, not utopian. It's right and true, that everyone should count as one, and no one more than one – and here you shape the kind of guy you are, and where you fit. It's not the good, this city's not eternal. It is my way of seeing things, things as they are.'

Outside, there's a line of police trucks. Odile says, 'My! I see myself in uniform,' and I think, 'You always are. Always at the top of it. Fashion.'

She says, 'Those must be the fiery chariots. Inside there is all sorts – you shouldn't fret. You could drive one of those.'

'No, I couldn't,' I say. 'It's not the guys inside, it's those alongside. Here, there's no modernity, it's all culture – that's what makes us fret and scratch.'

She says, ‘Finch’s idea is marvellous. No one pries – you’ve made your choice, and put yourself on show. Even subversives have their place, you just declare, and there you stand – it’s all administration, no more censors, you just tell them what you are, and all is firm and stable. He’s done the sums – there’s more than half of guys who just don’t care – one thing or another, peace or war, ho hum, they say, “We’re in our place, and life’s a grind for sure – but each is one and counts for one, and has a network that will care for them,”’ and on she goes.

‘I see no path,’ I say.

She pinches the muscle in my arm: ‘The path, the quest – it’s your invention, don’t you see? You could end up like Dea’s egg – you try too hard, the doctors have to rescue you, and put you in a shell.’

‘That’s crap,’ I say. ‘Things you invent are real – that’s how they made the axe, the wheel. The semi-automatic, paradise – it’s not a deviation, not a joke.’

‘Show me, then,’ she says. ‘Luca’s path – it’s all in books, we studied them, and didn’t take the path, and here we ended up.’

There is a pause. Dea in her egg, Mansour – his basket. Both destitute and living rough before salvation. Odile says, ‘The workers now – promoted, or they’re unemployed. That was some path that ended quick, that was the revolution past – how many turns ago?’

‘Just casuistry,’ I say, but don’t pursue.

I go on, 'Having no money is of no interest to anybody but ourselves. So, if we forget about it, that too's of no concern. No more than if we had a lot.'

'Or lost a lot,' says Odile. 'I'm dancing in the street. I keep up with trends, with culture too, and politics.'

'If what we wanted once had taken place, even quite exactly, it would have been a disappointment,' I say: 'The consequences. You can't wish for the unexpected, that always happens, and it's bad for you, for everything. Let's look at what there is – at Finch's plan. The modelling – it's exactly like a model farm, for beasts. A beast declares itself, it knows its place, its diet. A lion, a sheep – there's no mistaking them. They do what they can and must. In Finch's plan, the guys declare themselves – and put themselves upon his farm. They're animals, of course, they do what they can and must. But there are rules – and categories – that other animals don't have. It is a super-zoo, humane, because there are no visitors.'

'Except Finch,' says Odile, anticipating me. 'But he's a visitor with a stick, a net – but not for poking or for trapping, he puts you in the Gutter or the chariot. He is the law, the rule.'

'And not the path,' I say.

'And it's not a farm, you're right – on farms, the animals grow, the more they grow, the more they're eaten,' Odile says.

'They don't eat each other as a rule, on farms,' I say. 'Here, the guys consume each other, for there is no other nourishment.'

*

Analysis goes on. It's inconclusive. Luca says, 'Farm or zoo – there is a difference, you know. And where is memory in this? Nowhere. Finch's scheme aims blindly at the future.'

Well,' says Odile, 'you usually decide to forget what you don't want while you're going through it. Good things get nailed on, instead.'

Luca is sceptical. Odile says, 'I follow the culture, Luca. The modelling, it addresses itself quite clear. It's everywhere, in all its forms. Everyone is doing it, and betting on it too.'

'Everyone follows the culture, there is nothing else secure, Odile,' Luca says. 'It's the thing that moves, here, now. It's a fetter. The Future – it's a cloud.'

With Luca there are many silences. He makes full stops for you. Your mind is calm.

Odile says to me, 'Don't you want to be an animal? You just decide which one, and there's the rules. Then, you just stand around. Chat to your netted friends – so, maybe you're a fish. A free fish.'

I say, 'It's just a plan. Finch in the past was no obsessive, now he's up a step. Cops, model citizens. It quite makes sense. Bad guys are frozen out.'

Odile says, ‘I hear Finch deals only with the Gutter, and the fiery chariots. Seems there’s flaws, somewhere, in all the rest.’

I say, ‘I’ll start work soon. I’ll drive a truck, just like you said. Or I could be repetiteur – the opera, I know how they go. ‘My brow it is with laurel bound’ – I heard it all with Finch.’ I hum along.

She says, ‘What you said about those shoes is true – they take them off the poor so’s they won’t wander round.’

I say, ‘Of course – things come around, they’re all joined on. You break a leg – the join is always plain, the hurt, that goes away sometimes.’

## Coda

‘Luca,’ I say. ‘I need your help with Dea.’

‘No’, he says. ‘Help is one thing, requires commitment and exposure. What you want’s assistance.’

‘Give it, Luca, anyway,’ I say.

*

‘Cast me down, oh cast me down, and let me float, – away, be born again, be born as new, as something new,’ says Dea from her egg.

We trundle her wheels, her trolley, to the edge of the drop. Quite like the egg I didn't loot, before the revolution. She shimmers, and you see the veins, like little wings, green, purple, wriggling in the white.

'Oh cast ...' and down she goes.

She ought to hatch, as she drifts down. And –

'Yes!' I shout. 'I think I see – that huge dart of red and blue, that springs away, and soars and trills, and wheels and slides against the sky – for sure, it's something new.' I shout again,

'Luca, Luca – can you see – Dea is born, she's hatched, away she flies ...'

He says, 'You had your chance with her. You passed her test, sort of. And no, I didn't see a hatch, just that white bundle bouncing down – and there it is, all crushed below.'

I say, 'Luca, you missed it – that is just the shell, maybe a slice of white that's not consumed – the yolk is turned into a bird, an eagle, albatross – we'll see when it comes swooping back ...'

Luca is dry – he says a bird that size would need to feed on cobras and constrictors – or maybe Dea is a dragon and a maiden both at once, internal battling to the death. Since he's seen nothing, maybe the fall consumed her. On he goes.

'This casting down,' I say, 'it's only a technique. Let's try it on Mansour.'

Mansour is eager, and we wheel him out. He says that as he drops, his limbs will fall into their place again, the missing bits will reappear and all join up, and he'll alight, and walk back up, and greet – 'My one regret,' he says, 'is not to make it in the movies. Though they are coming to an end, and gone all bland, transported beyond our lives to places that we can't afford and shouldn't like, with snippy divas and dull guys who pleasure them behind the screen – ah, what a history, what end so premature the movies had!'

Instead, he's manacled, a suspect: on him is stencilled THIS GUY IS PROPERTY OF INSURANCE CORP but you can hardly say he's been a worker for the industry, though vital to its interests.

His basket runs on wheels, and Luca says to him, 'With Dea – we have had epiphany. So with a happy spirit, we shall toss you down, and you'll be whole, the rope trick in reverse, the stunt no longer stunting,' and he's trundled to the edge, and down he goes, each several bit goes separately. He sings – some part of him – that aria, 'my brow's with laurel belted round', the favourite of Finch.

'Well, Luca, where's he gone and ended up?' I ask.

'He was a hopeless case, in life, in injury,' he says.

We turn away, we don't look down. The miracle – if one there was – unseen.

*

We go to Finch again, Odile and I. He's making history, that is our excuse.

‘Well, here you are again,’ he says, quite cool.

‘We’ve sorted out the other two,’ I say. ‘Our friends and yours. Dea – turning into something new. Mansour, who is as he was, his condition is now permanent, decisive too, symmetrical again,’ and Finch just smiles. He says,

‘Here, we’re all coming to that point – the ancient questions asked with urgency: “where do we go?” “Who holds the goad, the bag of carrots?” “Where’s the good life?” “How do we stop our neighbours making slaves of us?” And Capital: there’s lots around, it seems, but not so much for us to buy that isn’t toxic. The globe is big and round, but things slide off, the friction’s heating everything, we fry – but that you know. And here you are again, to watch me make good lives for all the people here,’ and Odile’s in a mood. She says,

‘And how banal, good Finch, to model everyone, and dodge the questions ...’ and he’s angry, and he says,

‘It’s true, the figurines are small. Adjustment, cancellation needed all the time. But they are not belittled – that, yes, would be banal. Besides, you understand, the figures are a sample, only, of the whole. Where everyone is stored, is in computers, like elsewhere. To start with, Gutter and the fiery chariots – those are my immediate concern,’ and Odile’s at him once again, she says,

‘You guys all turn to fascist tricks. The world is drifting to its end, instead of letting good guys have their say, you spend your cash on fiery chariots. We end up in your Gutter, you make the good guys pay to keep us miserable and quiet, and wear dank clothes and eat the stalks of things.'

She's right, and Luca's lesson's coming true, though it's too late, and ranting is not opportune, and irritates good Finch. He says,

'I'll take you up a bit, and you can see the good guys having fun and making things and chilling out. All is maybe not the good life, but it's not the bad.'

So, there it is, a little plane, it's like it's made of tinfoil, and the air is all around, and seats for two. Finch sits behind, he flies the thing, Odile and I cram in before. Some guys have pushed us to the edge, the launch – the motor's soft, inaudible. We're off – we drop, then forward, like a miracle, we fly, we zoom, we're all tied in. The plane twists round, it gyres and spirals like a triskele, or a sycamore pod – the motion is unusual. We're with the birds. Then we see, below – the miniature.

It's Finch's floor, as far as you can see. It's all alive, the squares with babies pushed in carts, the roofs with nude guys hanging clothing out, the cats, the camels, clumps of guys that's arguing, big demos – there's the red ones, there's the black, and there's the fiery chariots all dashing up and down. And further out there's farms and zoos, and guys on donkeys being rough to other living things – and towers and spires and minarets – we hear the call to prayer, the bells, the gun that tells the hours. Here is a model Vatican, basilica with a pope sat on the steps, dressed like a red ant. Guys around, with flags. And there are slaughterhouses, and carpet discount sheds, and reservoirs of fried-out oil, and places where they make the string for tying sausages – and on and on, enormous, a hundred times the floor of Finch's shack, where we were featured as his friends, and now he has a million friends, tiny and gesticulating. Maybe too, his cat, his horse.

Odile says, 'It's all illusion, underneath these piddling things, there's something big, that is not shown – it can't be. Capital is not displayed, nor guns that kill a guy with thirty shots, nor freedom, being left alone, and such,' and Finch is angrier still, and throws the plane around the sky as if it is on wires, and there's no sound – it's not a glider, but it doesn't seem to have a motor, maybe it doesn't run on fuel, and Odile's getting restless, we're both squeezed up, she shouts that Finch is violent, like paternalists in general, and he says,

'My dear, it is the culture, what can you expect?' but she's not done and as she shouts, her spittle wafts back in his face, he says,

'My dear, all government's too harsh or too incompetent – it comes and goes like that, and mostly it is both, harsh and incompetent, but after all – it rises from the culture, what can you expect?' but she is not appeased, she blames him for his doing and his not, and keeps repeating how he should have learned his lessons when we were with Luca and all of us were friends, but now ...

To drown her out, he hums, 'now is my brow with laurel girt,' and seems to think a gesture is required.

He grasps the little banner on the plane, sets it alight, and casts it down. It's late, and darkening now. The flame flares out, a candle in the gloom, it flickers, falters, then it ends, a stick is all that's left. We don't see where it finishes. 'There,' Finch says. 'My friends down there will know I have a plan for them. Benign, of course,' and shouts rise up to us, of friend, of foe. He says,

'I know these theories – French, they mostly are – how life is dwarfing guys, and turning them to beasts or mere illusion – for purposes of gain and sadism, or worse. But now, Odile, you're down, the trip is over. Time to get out,' and we are both relieved, it's crowded in this seat, and windy; saliva uncontrolled is whipped about – the motion, and the twists ...

Odile steps up on the seat, and now I see – she's wearing yellow pants – and she's coordinated! The ivy and the cranberry, the tennis shoes – yes, it was the blue jeans, not the bomber jacket, that's what made the colours squawk – now, she's quite a picture, harmony, all's resolved. She's less irresistible, that's true – but though she has a jagged tongue, her colour sense comes right.

She jumps down, without a sound. She's angry, there's no doubt.

'Oh no!' says Finch, 'that's terrible. I didn't mean 'get out the plane' – we are a hundred metres up, or more.'

I look – and so we are. 'Yes, yes,' I say, 'quite terrible! She's gone. An accident, for sure – communication's let us down.'

'With all those arguments,' Finch says, 'we hadn't noticed it was dark – the smoke down there as well – it quite obscures the distance that you need to jump. These little planes – we get them secondhand, I think. But after all, I always felt Odile was not quite right for you – you sidle like a crab through life, and she went straight ahead, just like my horse. A kind of tunnel speech, she had.' He laughs, and then, 'Of course, I shouldn't laugh. But then, you didn't plan, or even have, a family, you two, and so there's no one to be told. Ah, families – mine is so big, it does for both of you; and you, my friend, face no expense. A funeral – it costs so much ... ah well, that is the culture, what can you expect? It's memory, it binds us all. That's what I revere – the people mostly come by chance, but when they go, it's mostly planned, as you must know from Dea's case, poor Mansour's too – intention's always for the best, and as you know, there is no way to judge intention, it is a thing extraneous to moral law and philosophic discourse ...' On he goes.

*

I remember Odile said, 'Drive a truck,' and 'Find yourself a woman who's not me,' advice I'll maybe act upon, though now Finch is talking about memory again, of how he laid our friendships on his floor, part of his life, although it's something of a bore when people from the past return. I say,

'Remember – we went shooting,' and he brightens, and he lands the plane, and says,

'That was the best of moments, my old friend. You were up there, with me, at the peak of things. No friend could ever have done more.'

# Sinking the *Aurora*

'La flamme est un monde pour l'homme seul'
Gaston Bachelard, *La flamme d'une chandelle*

'SHAKE THE TREE, shake the tree! Strength, more strength! Shake it, tumble them down – the prophet perched up there, the spyglass boy, the golden apples, and the pheasants! Hear the roots creak! See, down it all comes, trees are made for this, grow tall and fall.'

'Are you awake?' I ask.

On the wall, the tv set, we keep it on, alert all night and every night, our candle, sometimes candle-flares, no sound, but wriggling like a brain. Its throat, for the moment, is tied.

She says, 'Survival, making it through. Finding a customer, doing a trade. A minimum of curiosity. They say we've so much cold here, we ought to cage it, pack it, send it off to somewhere else. Ship it off. Cool hot places down.'

‘That sounds hard,’ I say, ‘if not impossible. Besides, survival isn’t up to us. It’s best to travel, slick, fast as you can.’

She says, ‘That’s you! In your nutshell! You must push it, heave it, till it breaks. You can’t slide, everything resists.’

I say, ‘You’re too good for me, Gabrielle.’

Her little imperfections, the nose – a hint of fingerbone...

‘What’s good to do with it?’ she asks.

I mean – destructive, strong. Cutting at the roots.

‘You’re sweet,’ she says. A moment too late. ‘You know, I want a certain moment of you. You, but some time past ...’

I say, ‘You can’t do that, that’s movies.’

‘OK,’ she says, ‘I want you in an old movie, with old sentiments.’

On the TV there’s a tiny man, he’s running and a guy behind is chasing, hits him with his stick, and makes him drop.

Looks like a service baton, and she says, ‘They’ve been going on all night. He never gets away. He never quite makes it, where he’s running to. Freedom, dignity, they say. It’s the politics that’s following, catches up. They say it is modernity – makes you wonder.’

Those two are in a hot country, there are leaves, a cactus. Here, outside, the fog is like a barricade. I say, ‘Today, I drive the truck with Piotr, down to Moscow.’

She turns over fiercely, and I think she sleeps.

*

I leave Gabrielle sleeping. She's noncommittal in repose, absent, the anger boiled off, maybe distilled and bottled, sold off somewhere.

She says I'm quite the passive type, don't care too much who is in charge, some order, or some clan. She thinks it makes a particular sense to me. She thinks here, here in the permafrost, it's all precarious. They've wired the buildings, conduits, gutters, all will be blown when there is trouble. Or else the gas beneath our feet. The buildings shift, unease all round.

Now, she dreams, perhaps. Things being born, profusion of warm travelling things that reproduce, that eat each other. Things with keen eyes – eyes round and yellow, eyes like lentils, stripy marbles: ridged like cones. Up and down eyes, left and right eyes. No trick missed.

The truck. Away, away! To sacred duty, work. A chore that lets me change the scene. I think of this and that, and walk the street – and there! I've fallen, holes in the fucking street. It's good that no one helps me up, they just skirt around.

A fog of ice and snow, the cold makes buildings creak and crack. Guys wearing all their clothes. Thaws, when they come, that smell of excrement. Better off without.

Cop waiting for some traffic, purple in his purple coat. Unmeasurably cold.

Piotr, my mate is here, he says, 'It's day. It's white, so now I'll drive, and when it's black, it's night, and up to you.'

There's weight of something in the back. We're doing two hundred in the snow – 'White is not purity,' Piotr says, leaning out the cab, confirming that the wheels don't turn: 'This shelf slopes down to Moscow, so we slide, just the initial push, we're off, the wheels don't turn. Mountains? Do you see any?' And I don't.

'Ah, Scotland,' he says. 'Those dinosaurs in the lakes. They live a hundred years, a solitude. At night, when no one sees, they go off mating. Over the hills, another lake, and just one baby! Eats its parents, just like us – that why there's no skeletons. Better not go out at night,' and he laughs.

Piotr keeps us rolling on. He's other universes up his sleeve, he beats me at cosmology – his eight dimensions beat my five, his pocket's filled with galaxies. He says he's quite indifferent, when we arrive, he'll turn around and back again, and so, and so. This time, it isn't so.

'It pays quite well, this trucking – there's nothing you can buy,' he says.

We eat some fish, exploded as you trawl them up from far below, the dark – you drop a light, they follow as you draw it up, they think it is the sun they've never seen. And – pouf! – it's revelation, over quick and sure.

We stare at each other, black tails sticking from our mouths, it's all a marvel, then it's whoosh! we're off the track, but on we go, and faster still – it's ice.

I drive all night, he drives all day – by dusk, his eyes are white, all white. We drive, we slide, all night, at dawn my eyes are black. You need a candle flame, you stare – and back they come, the naturals, the human eye, its white, its round of black. There is a sun, sometimes, pale as a yolk. I've never seen a moon. The fog is black by night.

'These tubes,' says Piotr, nodding back to where they lie, great khaki stoppered things like trees, 'is full of special gas. Heavy, it is, like lead. They store it in the clay.'

He sees, 'In the white, lines of white people, not carrying, not pulling loads, just walking. Fast as they can.' I ask,

'Do they look up? Wave? Cry out?'

'No, no, it's all quite silent, and we go so fast the other way, I don't suppose they'd notice us.'

He sees these people, in the black I see black shapes, like pustules or like cut-outs, black on black – it's quite unlikely. Nothing is nothing, after all.

'Let's see your passport,' Piotr says. 'Yes, that's a good one.'

I say, 'You need it to get anything. It's odd, unless you've got one, they don't let you out. You'd think they'd be delighted … We'll get to see your son, a presence positive, I'm told,' I hope I'll never see the lad, a nasty piece of evil's work, and Piotr says,

'He's not got hope, he's got conviction. Keeps you on the level,' and he's proud, proud they've survived the history, the life, the metamorphoses, the changelings, and now to be out of each other's way. Kicking up their legs as they're set free.

'You see,' says Piotr, 'this black and white – poor devils in the white, your pustules in the black – it isn't good or bad. Remember movies, once all they had was black and white, no red or grey, nor purple even – they weren't about the good or bad. It's just the vision – into the black, you see for ever, the white, it's so frustrating ... there must be something there, you think, and yet those people, they're so wispy. The black – it just goes on and on, no obstacle.

'It's in the white you slide along, and bang! – a wall, a cart, a bit of axle fallen in the road. You hit. The guys, the ghosts, don't care a bit. You're done for.'

I say, 'It happens in the black too,' and he considers, slowly, chewing a bit of fish. At last he says,

'Yes, that's true too. That's exactly what I said. Old movies.'

'We're the last two free animals,' says Piotr, as he locks the cab. Leaves the candle. 'The last two, probably, in the galaxy.'

'How'd we get back,' I ask. 'Uphill?'

'We don't. We leave the truck, the heavy gas that maybe no one knows exactly what it's for, and so is precious beyond words. We split the money given us for fuel. The bread and fish – enough for both. And then – more freedom still, quite unimaginable. Expanses – see them open up beneath your feet, like the savannah. like the steppe, the tundra, the heat, the cold ...'

He captivates me. Can two guys start a civilisation, a tribe?

'No, you idiot,' he shouts. 'We haven't bonded. Each his own way. Walking. My backside's flattened out, it's tinned and tooled.'

So, we stand there, his is a recipe for staying poor and losing everything. and starting the journey over and over, luck is the fuel. It's not for me.

The white road's turned to black. Here's the compound – 'let us in' we cry. We leave the truck there, Piotr throws the keys up, up in the white. If they fall, it's inaudible. Now locked inside, the candle! Opened our eyes and set them right, our black and white. Our duty's done.

*

'You get power – it means you're responsible for all this shit,' says Piotr, out of nothing.

'I don't want power,' I say. 'It's all armies anyway. I want to get away from Gabrielle. She's a pure spirit. Angry with it all – police, the frost, the black, the white. That's why I drove the trucks. Now, just give the money over, I'll be off, Piotr, good teacher, friend.'

'Money?' he says. 'There's no money. It's vouchers. We'll need someone to take them. Anger? Gabrielle – the nose, the chin, too sharp, skin like an embalmer's ad.

Hmmmm. Anger's not bad, but you see, there's no red here any more, no grey. They've tried to change everything, many many times – workers, peasants, nations, war and peace. Now, it's all army types, whatever else they say. It's purple, black and white.' As if reminiscing, he goes on, 'My son, Fyodor – he's into gangs, and marching up and down. And dressing up. And lipstick – doesn't mean a thing. He's angry too, but easier to live with – often he don't come home. And he's powerful friends. But vouchers – they're the devil,' and he shakes his head. 'Maybe us – people – shouldn't try to live together. Sad songs. Wolves that wait for you as you come off the sledge. Pushed or slipped.'

We contemplate our future.

'Why'd you end up in the frost?' he asks.

'Pioneering curiosity,' I say, though that's just a fraction of it.

'Places that's hard to get to, and to leave – it's because they're not worth it,' says Piotr wisely: 'There, you expect to get kicked about a bit.'

*

'It's not about football,' says Fyodor, Piotr's son. 'It's about winning. Your team.' Maybe it's a metaphor, this football. 'Some losing is inevitable, and that's the spur. It's knowing that nothing's final,' and he's pleased with himself. If I had some contact, a hair from someone, a brush against a bit of faith that clings, belief, an image of my bit of land – I'd smash his stupid face, and send him far away. But – what land? Sick sheep, a rusted tractor. Wisdom? Vision? The long drama?

They're like monks, these guys, living a full homosexual life, without the sex. Instead of sex they fight, or shape up to each other. Black tape binds up the rips, the wounds, careful with weapons, they're like vintage cars. Yes, I could do all that, and boss the weaklings, make them do for me the things that make life not so hard, but not so soft. It's mini-combats, miniatures. No big pictures here, no big day, just practise to be heroes, all in a bunch.

'Piotr,' I say. 'I'll never be a football fan. A fighter, a guerilla. I understand it all, the rectitude, the project,' and he says,

'You haven't understood a thing. It's all much smaller. Bullying. Being frightened. Little things you want to save – your plot of land. It's all quite small.' I must have missed the point.

Piotr says, 'My son – it's all right, as he's small. The bigger things, they just don't enter.'

*

Fyodor snaps at me, 'Don't stereotype me.'

'But you're typed all over,' I say, and he is. Crosses and swastikas and dates and wriggling things, suns in blue ink. 'That's wisdom,' he says, 'Sometimes just knowledge.'

Here's a sword, a locomotive, something from Motörhead ... I say, 'I can read you like an icon,' and he laughs.

'You're a comrade, a *camerata*,' he says, and here's his wild bunch, guys taking off their tops, now white and lardy, topclothes hanging down like bustles.

He grabs me, 'Look, look, you blind fool!' and points, and there it is, a yellow cross, five metres high. Atop, a little dangling thing, a guy quite naked, head drooping down like a dead kitten's, that thin neck ...

'Simeon,' says Fyodor, 'got crushed. So now we'll send him up,' and it's like Mexico, the cross that sends you straight to hell – a good position there, and merited no doubt. We wave goodbye to Simeon, and now there's flame, orange and black run up the stem. 'A sign,' says Fyodor: 'Vengeance.'

A guy in front, wearing a kind of smock, 'Oh,' he shouts, 'clap your hands together, all ye people,' and they do, and the heavy music starts, but I hear the voice: 'gone up with a merry noise', and here it comes, the sound of the trump, the trumpet. Here's the trumpeter, another guy makes a drum out of a box, and up the dead guy goes, all flames, and doesn't even crackle. Now cops are jostling round, must be believers too –

Those cops – they push us into vans, Piotr and me too. It hardly hurts, and now we're off, some naked guys like plucked turkeys on the floor.

Far off, the cross is black, a smudge of barbecue on top. I ask, 'Where – what's all this?' and some guys says,

'The pit. We do a battle with the other guys, the southerners. The fans. The other side.'

'It's not my fight,' I say. I'm scared, and Piotr too, though he's got a family link.

'Forget the voucher and the keys,' I say. The cops don't listen, they don't care. They're in a cage up front.

'The game, the game! *Igra, igra*,' they cry. I'm pushed aside, a cop says, 'You're for after,' and Fyodor's guys face up to the other guys, the southerners. If our guys lose, the cops will sort things out. I say to Fyodor who's beside me, 'You should be fighting too,' and he says,

'You enjoy being beaten with rough sticks?'

His hat – 'It's sable', he tells me, looks like a pearl on top, and the cape – isn't that black fox? I say,

'It doesn't look like Moscow stuff,' his gloves are round his neck, they're big, like boxers', hold maybe a pint of vodka each. He says offhand,

'It's all scum here – my guys, the other guys.' They're swinging with their laths, more carpenters than samurai. He sneers a bit. I think he's drunk as well.

'I dress to style,' he says. 'It's China. Not the guys that's now on top, but those that were – imperial.'

His eyes are full of Chinese winters long ago, the altar of the silkworms, all those uniforms, the clothes, the concubines. The hat – looks like a tsar's, but he sees it as Chinese. He hugs his father, Piotr pulls away. There's shouting from the scrum, some guys make daggers from their sticks – there's guys that's lying hurt, the celebrations come and go.

'Is this the best?' asks Fyodor, 'Our guys. The southerners. Is this the best, some grappling in the mud?'

They put the southerners in vans, and for the rest there is a bus. Some cheer, and some have lumps on heads. The cops have gone, and as I walk ahead, in front of Fyodor, there is a bang! It can be only him, who's hit me on the head ... I turn, he's got a plank, I give a little scream, and 'why the fuck'. It's bleeding now. Piotr stands aside. The consciousness – they write so much and talk about – in my head it's swirling round, pain and confusion, indifference except to what I feel. It's not worth much.

'That was a plank,' I say to Piotr, but he looks away, and Fyodor just laughs and says it was a gift, a gesture, maybe it just slipped – 'Enormous sausage, monstrous salame, leapt up as I was gifting it.' So, where's it gone? Perhaps the cops have taken it – how come there's splinters in my wound? He says,

'No one's exempt. It bonds, the pain. Yes, there's always more of them, the southerners, but they are subjects too, like you. You all play the game,' and on he goes. I ask,

'Where'd they get taken to, the losers?'

He says there's always other games, it's discipline, restraint, it's like the Romans, the civilised against the rest. The gladiators – that's how we remember Rome ... and what was that all for? It seems that life is boring if you're unemployed, he says, and boring too if you have got a job, so gaming fills the afternoons, or gladiators, it's universal and a sign of prosperity, of taming holy nature. He says,

'If you don't want that, don't want to play, you'll see you'll suffer all the same,' and so I say I know all that, and someone's stole the vouchers, so it's simpler now, we've just to get away – here come the cops, and questions come – identity and purpose, things we're all unsure about. And so the hours pass away.

'What do you want to know?' I ask.

'How can we tell?' says the cop. He carries on. I think of Gabrielle. She's curious about the cold, how people want to live where no one should. Now, she'll be curious about me, where I went. She wants a full life – as if it matters, when it empties out. Full of what? Of memories? They linger. The cold – that lingers too. No bright birds, no yellow silk.

Epiphany! The heavy gas! I shout, 'You want to know what use it is?' and there is relaxation, expectation, some guys rush in to hear, and others get pushed out.

'Ask Fyodor,' I say, and someone says, 'He's one of us.' I tell them,

'It's precarious, the moment is a shaky one,' the cops all nod, as if they're holding up a dying thing, that when it croaks, it falls and surely it will crush them too. The funeral, with servants sacrificed, spading deep the frosted earth you find the shaggy elephants ...

Ah yes, the gas, ah yes. I say, 'It stabilises. The palaces, the seas. The sun, the moon. These things that's falling down – you pump it in. It even works with presidents, and bodies of armed men. Cities go sliding down, the continents are on the move, they ride up on each others' backs, the seas rush in and out. Gas. That's what you need. Stability.'

I am the man of revelation – not the archaic kind with good and evil, whores of Babylon and such – but practical. Avoid the dreadful end, the last and everlasting things. The place where it all ends and just runs out, as if you'd eaten it.

Cops, armies, and intelligence – of course you need them, more and more, and everywhere, and all join in, forget the rest, bright birds and yellow silk, the rest is whimsy – but you need a base. That's where our gas comes in.

*

'Not a salame,' Piotr says, 'I saw it clear. A mortadella. Gift, I'm sure.'

I repeat, 'A plank, old friend.' But no, Piotr's turned, he's of the sausage persuasion now. Well, all is past, I've picked the splinters out. He says,

'You walked out on your girl – for that you'll suffer.' Then he rears up, 'I do not betray. I'm good. I'm good as buttered toast. With cream, with cheese, with what the fuck you want. Till you've seen me, you don't know what goodness is.'

Maybe he's right, I try it out – 'A plank,' I say.

He says, 'I must be good to everyone, and one of everyone's my son. Goodness doesn't choose, you know, or else it slides off to the bad, and I was good to you, when our truck was sliding down, and I'll go on like that. Being good. You must be satisfied with that.'

He brings out a picture of Fyodor, and there's the boy, on rollerblades, down the potentates' traffic lane, arms out, an angry bird.

'You're surely not his father?' I say.

'I never said that,' Piotr says. 'But he's my son, I chose him. Even some creation there,' and I say,

'Maybe beneath it all, he's a good lad,' and Piotr, angry, says, 'There's no beneath.'

We're silent. All around is bricks and sticks. The cops have gone. A sign says 'Las Vegas', but there is no desert here.

Then Piotr says, 'It's a terrible thing, not to love the dead. Though I suppose – if you leave someone sleeping, you can always go back.'

I say, indifferent, 'Gabrielle's a sour pickle. Just when you don't want it, too.'

Fyodor strolls up. Style puffs him out. I say,

'I like your plan – presenting some quite new personage. Not a celebrity, you're rough as bricks. You don't entertain – can't sing. No great ideas. Just presence. Some magnificence. Millions are waiting, just for this. Perhaps. Chinese. New empire from the history books, that no one knows. Your own militia. Sporting stuff – game that lasts to eternity, like tapestry, the inarticulate with magic feet ... And you, above it, dancing master without qualities, just flitting up and down. Yes, you cover everything, like spring paint. That scowl! That face in Chinese white!'

He turns his eye on me. I ask, 'What shall we label you? Warrior, streetfighter, star? Rapper? Bringer of good and evil?'

'No,' he says. 'None of those.'

'Internet marauder? Androgyne? A name? Explorer?'

'Yes,' he says. 'All of those. But now – I need a driver, a donkey.'

I'm disappointed. I say, 'Try your father,' and Piotr snuffles irritation down his stumpy nose. Fyodor exclaims,

'No, no! Here's apocalypse again, and my father's driving me? That spavined mule, those drooping legs? It's time to go, I'll gallop down the sides of the ravine, the heat is on me, I sell off all possessions, packed in plastic bins ... I go down south to meet the guys, maybe my enemies, maybe they'll love me, all those masses – and I need a driver! A feisty face, no sentiments, no ties.'

The fard. The tassels. And the furs. He could be a lovely boy, a rather podgy girl. Those Chinese emperors – did they die in battle, wearing all those clothes? Or send a servant, doing it instead? And – see where it all ended. I say,

'I see you rolling through the world, and gathering, sweeping up, the impotent, the wretched, all the guys that know the answers, can't do a thing with them and–'

'Yes, yes,' he interrupts. 'I'll be in on that too.'

'Are you sure you know all about it?' I ask.

'Are you?'

Off we go, South, down the Military Road, with Georgia on our minds, bit uneasy, that – the road as I remember it, thronged with trucks, some losing pieces, swerving. We're in a van, a Seventies jewel, and 'Seventies is all the style,' says Fyodor.

It's steeply raked, with purple lovelights. Piotr's in the back. He snores. 'No, not my father,' says the son, 'A casual adoption, the best way, no poison in the genes, no mortality.'

He sleeps a little too, and blames it on – 'My diet. The bottled stuff, paprika, fish exploded from the depths – gaining their wisdom in the dark.'

I say, 'Stupid too, those fish, to swim towards the light,' and he goes on, he says that breaking with your dad should end psychology, biology, all the stuff that ties you down.

'I can't see,' I say, the rake's so steep I only see a metre ahead, but Fyodor is perched on cushions, and he waves to all. I hear the roadside guys – 'The Seventies! A time to be alive! Amerika!'

I concentrate.

'We're here,' says Fyodor, and here's a track, no South – some mushrooms broad as chairs, butterflies that swoop and hum, brocade. The birches, thin as faun legs, gold where the silver bark is blistered off. Nature daring: over the top, puts out a massive tongue, a furry one. And those are eyes beyond the reeds, wolves waiting for their season. Is that an elk? And here's the hut, tarred paper over sticks, a bad black egg. Here's chickens, some two metres high.

'We're here,' he says again. 'Open the kingdom.' In we step, myself the prince's counsellor plotting all ways, and Piotr, woken with a kick from dreams of lakes and randy lizards.

I don't want to go inside. 'Why this witches' hut?' I ask.

'There's a witch inside,' laughs Fyodor. Piotr's asleep again. 'Let sleeping fathers lie,' says Fyodor, then Piotr mumbles about eternal fires beneath our feet, they've burnt off the roots, and if you push a tree, down it will go like scenery, it's all a privilege, these country homes, no water and no light, that road that's full of trucks that's trucking same things up and down, and pirates stop you, and they take your stuff, and back it goes to warehouses that gets robbed and then it starts off down again, the Military Road, that's full of tanks that's going up and down, and full of holes and guns that dangle down like empty organs, some with a cross, the tanks, some with a scrawl, and then the carts that's full of serfs from long ago, tied up in bundles, dirty feet like doorhandles sticking out.

I see some guy has sprayed the van:

**MUSHROOMS ARE DEADMENS' HATS**

and it could be true, think of the rivers, poison flowing to the sea, the bushes with their paper lanterns, hotter than rubies.

'Come on in,' shouts the witch.

'Let's have an Inquisition,' says Masha the witch, 'and do bad things.'

So we do.

'I'll set the rules,' says Piotr. 'And I'll do the punishments,' says Masha.

She smells of good bottled things, but 'Good things go bad, they're better then,' she says, and so we eat bad fish and pomegranates – flesh of rubies warm and green – and think of bad things that the three of us can do. Piotr's the fourth, the judge. He sleeps.

'There is no hope, no goodness here,' says Masha, 'So it's all a slouch up to the scaffold,' and she smacks us with some twigs, and Fyodor enjoys it. Masha says Fyodor is come to save us all, he'll do the crimes and set the punishments on us – 'He wants to be a singer, he can't sing: he'll be an electric zombie like all the other bodies, can't live, can't die, would be an emperor, but he's not obeyed,' and Fyodor just winks, and she goes on, 'He's a costume, just a pair of pants, a puffed-up sausage skin,' and at that word, my head throbs out, and on she goes, she takes a cobweb and she scrolls it, makes a pellet, brown and grey, and gulps it down, the shadows creep up to the roof.

I eat and eat those bad fermented things, we do bad things and call up worse, and I don't think of Gabrielle at all, we're free, it's mutual, and Masha says Fyodor wants to set his seal on everyone, she sets an iron down in the heat, the peat is red and white with fire – I feel the cold, the tundra, sloughing off, it's good, and I say 'More, just more!' and Masha says beware of greed, and certain things need writing down and spelling out, and with the iron she brands us both, Fyodor and me, a sign that says 'adil', Just. 'Just what?' asks Fyodor, laughs and winks.

'Where are the days of hope?' I shout, and caper, down go Fyodor's sables and his little hat, I trample it, it crackles like there's bone, a skull, inside. And Piotr's slumping down.

'He's dead, he's dead!' I shout, and dead he is, it doesn't stop us prancing – for when you've done your years, well, out you go, and no one sheds a tear, you're an old umbrella, all blown out, dismasted with the wind from in and out, and Masha says we'll put him in the fires.

I shout again, 'The good, the good, that's what the Inquisition's for, it doesn't need to question and to pry, it knows the answer, doesn't need to talk. The answer is – the good,' and Piotr sprawls, he's judge and corpse, it's quite pretentious, but his son, his cod relation, Fyodor just sits, he's stewed and cooked, and ready to be bottled, and I shout again, 'The good!' and Masha says,

'You want the good? Here, it's these pickles, yellow and green, just like my eyes,' and that is true as true, and Masha is my universe, and round the wolves run, round and round outside, they've eaten those huge chickens, and the heat must fire their paws, nothing to do but run from hot to hot. And then we sing, and there's accordions, someone has brought a fiddle, and the hut is full of people, live or dead, who cares as long as they can hold a tune – and Fyodor just sits and beats a bone upon his knee, one eye is white and open – and if this isn't paradise, it's twelve times better, and I say,

'Fuck driving, and the slavery too, I'll make my way ...' and if that's up or down, it doesn't interest, and gulp the pickles down, and my! – they're good, and Fyodor sleeps again but Masha's eyes, they never close, and you can't call this dancing, it's not hugging though, she never looks at me, we're run together like the poison rivers, we're the mushrooms with the skulls beneath, and round we run like wolves, and round and round we spin ... the heat runs up our legs, it burns, we suck it in our lungs. The walls are made of bottles, good and bad, and then we pick up Piotr, he's a century old, he's seen the good and bad and done them too, he's like an old frock coat, we go outside and kick a hole, there's ash and fire, the red, the white, we thrust him down, and puff! he's gone. So, back inside, and there is Fyodor – *my!* that drum is tall, two metres high, and all around its rims there's tinkling things – he drums for us, and we prance round and caper up and down. It's paradise, or twenty times as good.

Ah, Masha.

Warm at last.

*

'The keys, the keys,' it's coming from the fire, it's Piotr, and I say, 'Those truck keys are no use, the ones he threw – we need the vouchers,' but he's dead and ash, the vouchers too.

'Into the van,' shouts Masha. There's many people crowding round, Fyodor is moribund. Must be his diet – 'Those pomegranates!' Masha says, 'He gobbled them down whole', and laughs, 'No room, no room, room only for the dead.'

I say, 'Into the van, only the living,' so on both counts we push Fyodor inside. We leave the Military Road – it brought us little luck. Now, here's a church – out come the old sharp voices, sweet as harebells. Candles aflame. Maybe steal one – there's the town gate, not so welcoming, there's the jail, an Isolator, and I say, 'Gabrielle's awake' and Masha says so what, if mine is guilt or curiosity, by now Gabrielle will have a reason for knowing what is what. I tell her, Gabrielle was never short of reasoning, she wishes people'd got their revolutions right instead of half, and Masha says half is just the size there is, and Gabrielle said 'shake the tree', all that and Fyodor is stirring, and he says,

'If you've perfection in your gaze, you can't be watching boots and footfalls all the time.' No doubt he's right, and sacrifice and suffering – they're in our bones, and there's infinity of candles we must light, the point is just to stop the bad guys, and make a lot of tiny perfect things.

The live ones in the back strike up a song, it's heroes and the tragic horse who'll lie forever by his rider's grave ... oh no! this road's a track, and dwindles out.

'The keys, the keys! We need the keys,' says Masha, and I say,

'No Masha, not keys, we need a road. Don't be so fucking stupid, so – disappointing. Those were truck keys Piotr threw, not the keys of heaven. Paradise is where we go to whenever we want, it's warm, it's hot, it's ten times better ...' and on I go, and Masha says,

'It's time for dancing in the snow again.'

*

We're in the 'Revolution Palace and Brasserie'.

Fyodor says glumly, 'Thieves and drunks. That's all there is. We need democracy.'

There's no one here besides we three, except the barman, Rustam. 'I love you, Rusty,' Fyodor says, embracing him, and winking at us: 'Where's the girl?'

'Working the sidewalk,' says Rustam. There's two stilled glitter balls, a tank of carp where floats the wooden battlecruiser, the *Aurora*. Mother of the Revolution, firing off its blanks.

'The Mongols got here, devastating,' Fyodor says, 'But by the time they got here, they'd turned Chinese. Emperors, too. They started off to bring the Buddha, but they took so long, when they arrived, they turned Arabians. Now – shake it all up, that's what we need.'

I think of Gabrielle. Shake the tree.

Masha is sceptical. She and Fyodor – they could be sisters.

'It's all in the cards,' says Fyodor. 'Clubs, like this club here. And hearts – they're vital! If you do well, it's diamonds in your shoe. And if you fail – it's spades. Digging. Holes.'

'It's a punishment, this,' Rusty joins in. 'You get the punishment, that makes you feel like doing the crime,' and Fyodor says sharply, 'You're not the first that's seen that, my old friend,' and he softens, 'For that is life, in life there's wisdom, otherwise – where is the point?'

I ask Fyodor, 'Do you own all this?' It's most unlikely.

He says, 'Nah. Some cop or something like. I sweep up the cash.'

Some guys in overcoats come in, sit at the bar, stick out their rumps. A woman is haranguing them, she stands behind. They don't turn round. Fyodor tells one guy, 'Hey, you can't bring tarts in here – we'll make some calls and see you right with some of ours, some dancing too.'

The woman goes on talking, persuading ... 'lots of the stuff, beneath our feet, we ship it out, the cold, the chill, and cool down where it's got too hot.' She turns to Fyodor, and says, 'Fuck off, you creep – I'll outsmart any tart of yours,' and on she rants, then Gabrielle (for it is she), she turns to me and says, 'Of course, you're lurking here! Just let me sell our tundra to these overcoats, and then I'll have my say with you.'

The guys in coats, they sink the first two hundred grammes of booze, and someone says, 'We need stability, not cold. Eternal life, not freezing is the goal,' and Gabrielle says that's on the cards, she's heard of gas that does the trick, down in the clay it goes, then nothing moves. Some guy, a colonel it seems, starts up a song, 'Fountain of love, fountain of life – I bring you two roses …' it droops, the song, it flickers out, the glitter balls spin round. They make you dream of diamonds.

We sit, far from the overcoats. Masha says, 'Now, let's get on with our Inquisition.'

'... destroy,' Fyodor is saying, not heeding her, 'Destroy every work of man in North Vietnam. That's what they said. Americans. Quite a Mongolian thing. That country – wasn't even ours!'

Masha goes on, 'Fyodor, my dear – informer, and adventurer. Where may this adventure be? What can you find, without laboratories? Maybe – holy nature. Saving some animals.'

She points at me: 'And you? The eye: study and learn. There's punishments in that – you come to like them, they're your bones. Idleness. Not adventuring, not Fyodor and history, watching the others run around like ants, like water leaking out. Tied to yourself – pah! what a bore, stranded on your tiny island at your birth. Hoping some savage catches wise fish for you, and strokes you till you sleep. Searching for yourself – that is some punishment. What a bore. And how we suffer for what our fathers did. If you're rich, you want identity, an alibi. The others run from it. Punishment. All around. Our flesh.'

'It seems punishments aren't handed out,' I say, 'They're all inflicted on us by our innocent selves. What's Fyodor's punishment?'

'Boredom – tiring of the silly people suffering, when you take their cash and twist their ears and steal their dog. The faithful love the football more than they love you. Frustrating.'

'And Gabrielle?' She's hectoring the pudgy guys, all lickered up, arguing – ice or gas?

'Screw her!' says Masha. 'One thing there is, is permafrost. She wants to drill it out and sell it off! Sell to those guys! She's carrion.'

I say, 'Well, if I'm the eye, I'll watch and when I've seen enough, I'll take the galley over, make you row like rats. And you, Masha?'

'I don't need do anything. I'm the Inquisitor. Now, I set the rules.'

*

The overcoats armwrestle, army versus the police, Intelligence looks on. Fyodor is shouting that the bastards never pay, and Masha says, 'Oh no! He's off to get his weapons. Sausages.' Then the girl comes in, a *koshka* of the highest class, wearing a lovely spotted leopard – Tina!

Masha pokes her broken glass at Gabrielle's left eye – I think, – what can that accomplish?

Tina takes off her leopard skin. It might be jaguar, or ocelot – some spotted cat. The guys are drunk, and here comes Fyodor with his plank, wide as a mortadella, and he spins it round, the cruiser's sunk, the glitter balls flash round and round, there's blood, and even brains, and we're all in the wrong, or wounded, except Tina – and then Masha says,

'Quick, quick! All underground!' And there's the ladder, down we go, all feet and fingers, must be quick and quiet, a stranger's tumbling down behind: it's danger, then – 'Here we are,' says Masha.

'It's sewers,' says Gabrielle, but she can't see, and Masha says,

'No, no, it's tunnels,' lit by a multitude of candles, invisible. We see there's marble walls, and copper rails, all that, it's luxury, and she explains that labour was abundant, talent too, 'This way to New York' and we're incredulous. She says, 'And then the others, poor guys too, dug from the other end. It all joins up, from China to Antarctica and back again, and some is lined with feldspar, some with ads for pills. There's animals and guys still hauling clay – sometimes you're pushed along in vacuums like they used to send you change in stores, sometimes there's guys that pick you up in palanquins. There's elephants that's found a refuge here, some hairy and some bald, for them it's home. And there are little trains that smell of candyfloss. There's serpents too, and if you're extra-wise, you'll pass them by – and here there's wisdom stacked up on the shelves. The old religions come to die down here...' and Gabrielle shouts out,

'And are we safe?' and she is desperate, her eye's attacked, and sacrificed, she's lost her clients with their coats, their trade, and Masha laughs and says,

'Safe? Safe! Of course not, you are never safe, there's armies up and down, and spies, all that, and tubes along the walls that bear intelligence. Somewhere the sea comes in, and there is fire and frost, the flames beneath my hut, and cold that's under yours, dear Gabrielle. It evens out, the hot and cold – it's not like life above, here you survive, hot wars and cold, there's no disease, the microbes shun this place. Here you can live and travel up and down the world – it's all last century, I know, but here the spite and daring's gone, bled out. A little peace there is, though sliding up and down beneath the world, – it's not so great,' and she fusses over Gabrielle's eye – she says, 'The eye is fine, it's just the blood,' and Fyodor says if it had been the eye, we'd hear it pop, and Gabrielle says, well, ok, an impulse, but watch it, young Masha, your eyes are fragile too. She's on the mend, her sight is keen – that's what they say. And then I think,

'Keep trucking, that is what I should have done, for now I'm slipping into crime, it's all around, it's in our bones.' With Tina we are five, and Rusty up above will keep the tabs and hold the fort but here's a colonel, following us, and that makes six, but Masha's rolling on – 'It's shelter here for corpses, invasions and defeats. There's vaults and prisons, guys who've been in silence here for fifty years, lives unimaginable, sometimes there is music too,' and Fyodor brightens, and he says, 'Songs! and stories!' And the colonel says,

'I can tell stories, with a song to go ...' and Gabrielle – she grasps it all – asks,

'What's to do with him, this guy? And why'd he follow us?'

Masha says, 'That is his job. Fyodor's his sleeping giant. The colonel's an example for all those guys who know the answers, and can do nothing with them. Wise guys,' she laughs. 'Now, he's a burden, though his overcoat – that is his useful part. Fyodor! your mortadella, your plank – a taste of that, and we'll be done with him.'

The colonel protests: 'No, no, I'll sing a song,' and his were those two roses in the club above, before we threatened, and that army guy got hit, and we squat down, it's music time, we listen, and I think – maybe we can start again and make careers, the lovely leopard, Tina, she can work for us. Then the colonel starts to sing, a sound that's like dried flowers – 'My voice, calling you with love and longing, breaks the silence in the dark night,' and someone weeps, and someone says, 'how apt'.

Gabrielle's insistent as a burr, she says, 'On quests, adventures and the like, there's always someone loses limbs and senses. But this guy here,' she points to the colonel, 'It's not his voice we need – his overcoat, instead. It's damp down here,' and on his fate we hover round, our eyes are set on life and death – and Fyodor thinks long and says,

'This guy will eat our food. Best to be done with him,' but we've no food, and Masha says a month's walk takes us to Japan, or Baltimore, down here direction's all the same, you take your chance – sometimes up there it's sea, or cherry trees, or cemetery. From shore to shore you sometimes go, and never see or hear a wave.

We can't decide. The colonel sings his songs, and maybe he'll be president, all's fortune.

'We have to eat and sell,' says Gabrielle. 'Is all. Not wander round down here,' though I'd quite like to go to Baltimore, but not for long, and Masha says you try for luck and magic and you mustn't hope too much, above all don't have kids, or you'll end like poor Piotr stuffed down in the peat. And Fyodor says that's rather slim advice, that if she knows the answers and the questions too, surely some larger theme should surface. 'Just like what?' asks Masha, who is miffed – I saw her break her glass before she poked poor Gabrielle, and 'knowing all the tricks?' she says, and that is her profession.

'The theme is army – owning lots of stuff,' the colonel, getting bolder, says. 'The presidents come and pout, and strut, but in the end, we own the food and drink, and stills and labels for the booze,' and on he goes, and Fyodor at last comes in and says, 'You don't own Rusty, that's for sure.'

'Rusty's an animal,' the colonel says, and the leopard lady, Tina, says her life is crap, and even starving with us all is better than she's had, and words are fired and slashed, we scream and shout, there's nothing here to eat, the booze is wearing off. 'My curiosity is rolled quite flat,' says Gabrielle.

At night we sleep wrapped up in Tina's skin. The colonel sings himself away to where he goes, a spray of Pushkin roses on his lips. He keeps his overcoat – we may decide that it should be his shroud. By day, we roam around, pop our heads, like gophers, every now and then, to see where we have been, and what's above. Food, too.

Gabrielle can smell the heavy gas far off – we don't go down that way – we've more stability than is good for us. It's providence that nearly took her eye, for she is sharper now, she's quite forgotten how I left – for here I am. She shows no rancour, though her face was slashed, and Masha says, 'Gabrielle, I've quite forgiven you,' although for what we cannot tell, but everyone needs some forgiveness, though it doesn't last.

At times we think we see some bones, it could be Piotr, though by now he must be ash. The keys, the vouchers. that is all another life. Sometimes above it's roots and gardens, or there's guys that run. Sometimes it's Baltimore. It could be all a movie set, there is activity – could be a march, it could be waves, or people flying on a screen, and small apocalypses in a minor key take place – nothing that you can't repair.

When we find a massive vault, an engine shed, basilica, we set up Fyodor, install him on a throne, and make obeisance. It keeps him quiet, and even happy.

We tell our tales, we sing our songs. The colonel's life is spared, we pull him on behind, from sacrificial lamb he grows to sacred ram. There's no need for our passports here, we make a blaze with them, this is our road – there are no tolls, we've no significance beyond the journey that we make. We start to glow with rectitude, our nationality drops off.

Here is eternal life, if that is what we want.

*

Where shall we go to be born?

Many have an untimely death – no one has an untimely birth. The determinant is time, but that's always passing, so choose the moment carefully, decisively.

No mothers or fathers – they get in the way, though you need someone to ferry you over the river, coming or going. And a candle to light.

Tina considers Rome, then: 'No, if you're as beautiful as me, they give you everything as gifts at once – I don't want that, cash with snappers round. I'd want a steady income, stable people, I'd try to be a woman, not a tart. Let us move on.'

And so we do.

We consider the world, how to make our way in it.

'China,' says Fyodor, 'for the food. But it's kind of clubby. New faces stick out.'

'America,' says Gabrielle. 'It's an Africa, but without all those countries. There's mountain people, and plainsmen, river people, desert people too.'

'No camels,' says Masha. 'I'm not going where there are no camels.'

I propose Iran, 'The architecture's just the best,' but Tina says she's known people who come from there, we don't have the money or the family.

I say, 'Let's think America – it's porous. If Fyodor takes off his makeup, he could be a politician. We could import the Chinese food. Tina can be his wife, maybe a mistress too, and he can run for governor. Gabrielle – you'd sell us houses.'

Fyodor says, 'Being a senator's more fun. More Roman, too.' I say,

'Fun is not the word. You want to stay away from those old guys, and cuspidors, and stuff,' and Tina says she'd rather have the cash than sex, whether as wife or mistress, and I say that Fyodor will dress right down, and treat her like a queen.

Masha is angry, and she says, 'We'll just be trees, trees in a forest – Russian trees, it's true,' and Gabrielle says that being trees is better than the tunnels, no one knows you're there.

Then there's the colonel. Maybe he can confess to all the world, and everyone will take each word as true, and so he'll sing and sing. Then, Masha turns on me, and says,

'That's us settled – you, what can you do? Driving a truck is nothing new to them Americans, I'll bet,' and I say, 'I'm the narrator, I make you all make sense, and say your piece, and hang together: – you're all the puzzle, I'm the glue, I make you stick together,' and she's not satisfied, she says there's many kinds of puzzle, she'll build a house herself, not buy one ready planned from Gabrielle. She says,

'It's true the colonel sings – but he's not one of us. And nor is Gabrielle.'

*

'Fyodor's a funny boy,' says Tina briskly. 'He's so attached to his tattoos. In America, it should be easy to reach the top. They have elections, all you need is luck and numbers – then you get the power. Tattoos may help.'

'All that sex,' I say. 'It must have been so hard for you. And boring too.'

'No sex,' she says. 'There's no money in sex, the money's in the booze, and watching how the dancers gyre. It twists your brain,' she does a few steps: 'I ushered in the clients. Nothing in my job was hard,' and she confides, 'I love to pour the drinks. In come these sour pickles, drink for half an hour, and then they're softened up, they coil like rope. It's such a laugh. It's magic, like Masha's bottled fun.'

I'm not convinced. I say, 'Fyodor has done the crimes – politics would be his punishment,' and Tina says it's culture, you adapt 'to any kind of politics. The detail makes you glow and sprout, you climb inside the system, like climbing up a tower. It's all just weather – some places hot, and others cold. You have an audience, you say just what amuses you, what turns them on. Or else there's no one, or a camera – you must adapt. You smell the smells – you say, "it's war: free booze and dignity". You make the speech, you see them start to rock, and on you go. You make the joint perspire and jangle – raise it, raise it! through the roof – throw down the tiles!'

'Sometimes they throw you off the tower,' I say.

'Of course they do!' she says. 'They always do, if you live long enough.'

She knows about it all. America. We walk around this town. 'That used to be a smelter,' says the colonel, and there's guys in clothes like clowns', that's selling dust, and dust is all around.

'We've got here late,' says Tina, 'Still, Fyodor could make it here. His Chinese ambitions – well, when he's president, who knows? He'll do a deal. No more the warring states.'

I'm at a loss. I say, 'Maybe that's a good result. Besides, it takes you years to climb the tree – two years at least to get the power. But Fyodor – he thinks in seasons, football – he'd be bored.'

Tina's thinking on, 'Being a mistress sounds like fun, but – concubine! Who wants that. Doing laundry. Especially his.'

How can we escape the plot we've laid?

A revelation. 'Tina,' I say, 'there's no worry. The colonel – he has all the dirt on Fyodor. When we get tired – who'd want to rule this place? – the hopeless and the smug, the dust, the rust, all that – the colonel's our reserve, card in the hole. If things go bad, we'll have him sing his song, "Darkness lies over the hills of Georgia". The darkness will come, lying over Fyodor too – and that is right.'

She says, 'That's blackmail,' and I say, 'That doesn't move me, Tina.'

'You idiot,' she says, 'he'll punish you, and then he'll punish me. Up on the cross we'll go. Or in the charcoal pit, like Piotr.'

We stare into our history, our candle flame. Then, she says,

'The things he's done, we say they're bad – here, they look good to all these guys. Football, police spy, parricide – this country floats on these.'

She is the expert, that is clear.

Fyodor, as president – he'll bring the Chinese in, there'll be one world again, and all these guys will clap their hands. It's peace and trade. Southerners and Easterners – we'll all be one – the only detail is – where is it best to be?

'Not here, and that's for sure,' says Masha.

We're in the bar and Fyodor's behind the wire, the cage where bands play, protected from the things that guys may throw. The band plays 'Fire' – it cools, the guys calm down, and Fyodor shouts out – 'I'm one of you, I'm bad, you needn't wait to find that out.'

It's Gabrielle who tells him what to say – 'Open the prisons.' Some guys cheer and others snarl. Then,

'We need you paintball heroes! No more the smelter, and no more the mine – you'll all join up, and in the army there's a place for everyone. We tell those foreign guys – that if they pay, them we don't attack. So – in the money comes, peace and democracy all round. You bet those countries vote to keep us out, calm and far off – we'll just look mean and count the bucks!'

And how they cheer, and Fyodor unhooks the mesh, he's unprotected now, and dressed right down, and then – apotheosis, for he pulls a string, and from his back unfurls a peacock's rose, a massive tail of red and green. The guys all cheer again, it's mystery and fun, hope, liberation – all you need when going to the bar, better than the best band they get here ...

*

'Fyodor,' says Gabrielle, 'You could be president for sure – a month or so, you know exactly what guys want, and I can write it down for you. No illusions, jut some steady cash. Those paintball exercises round the town will smarten up the drab,' and on she goes.

Yet Fyodor looks glum – he says, 'This town, it isn't worth a spit, the guys are going down and down, I'm feeling sick ...'

I say, 'The architecture?'

'That too. A dreg. D'you think I look a clown, all puffed up?' he asks.

'You need to be puffed up, to be a president,' I say.

'The guys here – they're bigots, everyone's afraid of everyone else. There is a set of rules – you shouldn't kill the others – but at home, they plot and plan. They arm.'

I say, 'It's their values. And they like seeing puffed-up people.'

'It's a punishment,' he says. 'Mortadella or plank, it's all the same. For doing what you shouldn't. Or just reminders.'

I say, 'The sausage doesn't leave the splinters. Then – there's your militia, beating up the southerners.'

'All punishments,' says Fyodor. 'We should not have gone. South. They should not have come – up North, to us. Just common sense – all of it is true.'

I shrink from him, and say, 'Gabrielle does the impossible things. She is an expert, sorts out the anomalies,' and he laughs.

'You have to leave her sleeping, else she's your chain.' I say,

'All that you say is true, it's just I can't agree.' He shrugs –

'We have to find a place where we can both be right. And drink from Masha's jars.'

We have to leave America, here we can't be content, although there's bits of everything – can't find the glue to stick, the picture on the box is missing that shows you how it ought to look when all is put together.

'It's the rage,' says Fyodor. 'Everyone has got it – punishment is given out, the rage goes on. I have it too – it keeps me fresh.'

The anger – as it all goes down.

*

The colonel's safe, he's told his tale, he is believed. He's back again, in the police, the primal job, truth unscrewed from all our secrets. So, we expect, deserve, the sudden blow. Guilt. It always works.

'The problem is, is memory,' says Fyodor. 'You must forget – you don't forgive, it gnaws at you. Your head – and Gabrielle, that eye that Masha poked. Forget, forget! You go into a bar, and you get slashed – there's no significance, it's punishments for crimes that no one knows, and maybe never were. With memory, there's rancour, rancour with the dead, with birth, with exploitation – all these histories, they fire it up, undoing what can't be undone. This country here,' – and he waves towards Wisconsin, 'It's no need to exist – but here the guys go on, about the grandfathers, who did this or that ... It's history, the things you think you did, that's worth remembering, that screw up the scene ...' and in his excitement, he pulls the string, the peacock's tail blooms out and droops. I say,

'There's maybe good memories as well,' though I'm reluctant, I don't quite believe. They're all ephemeral, the good, the bad, the memories, and I say,

'Memories, forgetfulness – they're much the same. A well. Somewhere. You throw the bucket down, you pull it up. Memory yes, memory no, perhaps a little. Memory – it comes in dreams, it makes you rage – the good, the bad, what you remember, or forget – what you would kill for, what you'd die for. It's all a picture at the bottom of a well,' and I go on, and Fyodor says,

'Maybe, my friend. I haven't thought it through. But if we have to travel on, we must forget. Forget your head. And Gabrielle – her eye.'

Later, Gabrielle says, 'I'm looking for a way to cut a throat.' I say,

'Masha's? You mean you're looking for a knife? She's just impulsive. Some people say that's fun.'

'Don't finnick and fillet, you know exactly what I mean. The way to cut includes a knife. And a throat.'

I say, 'And sucking me in too, then having to escape.'

'Naturally.'

Ah, love – it makes you an accomplice. All that blood! The shack, abandoned in the birch trees – everything that's under vinegar and under oil. Masha! – all that makes you want some more. Lots more.

I tell Gabrielle, Fyodor's withdrawn his China schemes, of being candidate. China will come, inevitable, without him. And he'd never be elected. True, we are citizens, on our passports it should say – but on them we were: profession – sailor. Residence – the ship, with nets that take no fish. Citizens of the world that's not. False. I say,

'Too many false memories, poor Fyodor. Moscow, seat of the caliphate. He likes to watch the people fight. His militia – righting wrongs, creating them.'

'He hit you,' Gabrielle reminds.

'Just settling his account with history. Philosophy too, maybe. It didn't interest him, if things were good or better – just enough to be convinced that he could stand, there, centre of the universe. Dressed fancy. Wrong tattoos, but smoke and music curling round. Reclining, wise.'

We enjoy the picture. I say, 'Once settled, those accounts, what do you do?'

She waits a second, then she shouts, 'You cretin! Mishmashing up all that last century stuff, the truth, the right – you mustn't get sucked into that.'

I say, 'Killing Masha would be quite a puzzle. Is it worth it – questions and colonels? Not much Pushkin there.'

We talk again of Fyodor. Gabrielle says, 'Fyodor won't be elected when the Chinese come – not even as an autoworker. These guys elect lots here, but some must make it on their own. Where might he end up? And his women? Concubines.'

'I can't tell, I hadn't thought,' I say. 'The guys here – they kill lots that's not covered by the constitution so you'd better hope you're in it,' and she says yes, everywhere it's documents that count, and Masha comes along and says if you read the labels who knows what excitements you will miss. And that's true too.

The colonel's fixed himself, but he was never one of us, and I think of those keys we lost, way back in Moscow. And the vouchers too.

Something new. That's what we need. A place that fits, that makes a statement. No cars, no language. No questions you can't answer. No cold. Benign decay. A pair of every animal, to guarantee tomorrow. No vertigo from building up and digging down.

Here, there's too much metal hanging out, pipes and cables in the air, cut off, like someone's pencil just ran out of lead.

Gabrielle says, 'Resolve the immediate, that is my idea. This new world – it's so tiny, I can hang it on my belt. Masha did me wrong, it's up to me to sort her out.'

'Masha deserves some benefit,' I say.

'You can't show that you're both just, *adil*, you and Fyodor,' says Gabrielle. 'Not in public. "No tattoos, no brand on your body" – that's definite, word of God, all that. Bodies are something pristine, unmodified. And – you've no personality. Can we can use you – for something, maybe?'

I say, 'We're not statesmen – we know what we think, and how guys in bars act and think. Guy and thug with that baton, on TV. Maybe the fugitive – he got away at last. Laid a trap, even. Everything ferments, Gabrielle.'

How she drives on, when she's awake, and any fondness disappears, taken from her, from you. Maybe some new thing is being born. I say,

'That Soviet Man – he was a flop,' and Gabrielle says,

'Leave that Tina well alone – she's all too human. Masha is not, and she is not for you, not either.'

*

Tina and I – walking down the road. She says, 'There's high life, and low life – and the sidewalk. That's where I feel at home.'

There's no sidewalk on this road.

The noise, the smell. How do guys here make their music? They're all bottled up in automobiles.

Then – it seems there's animals, racing down the road towards us. 'Tina!' I shout, and I think how animals don't communicate with us, not like they used to, share a bit of wisdom or anxiety, and I remember there are snakes that slide along, doing sixty an hour, with ease – and now the beasts are on us! where can they have come from? Stores? Menagerie? A movie set?

Well out in front, pedalling along, scooting – an ostrich. Tina shouts out – 'It's escaping!' and she throws herself towards it, on it – and she's away, there goes her leopard coat: it double-scares her ostrich. I shout after her,

'What do you want, where? If it's escaping, let it go, at least suspend your judgement,' and she shouts back, 'No, no, it needs protection, or they'll shoot them all,' and here's a zebra, catching up, it shies away, it's seen the leopard, Tina, on her bird. And there's confusion.

She's back: 'They have a strange smell,' she says, 'And they're not friendly, like they are in the cartoons. I can't imagine killing and eating one.'

'You're not a proper leopard,' I say. 'You've a big sense of helping, even if you don't know why, that stops you taking the chance to run away. You slowed the bird right down.' She says,

'Yes, I suppose they're birds, but they lack so much, they make you want to give them a hand. So lucky us, we can still run.'

As they raced off down the road, Tina flapping, holding her ostrich, I wondered – would there be a revolution here? So much democracy, nothing else to ask for, all these poor people, stacked up on shelves or in barrels in the cellar, waiting, convinced, forewarned, all armed – not to mention government, those forces, the cops, the systems in the banks. Raise a hand against ... there's no one following. Yes, this is the future, the destiny, all running done, no point in asking, the tree well shaken. There's aliens in the movies, killing everyone – it's the battle, Armageddon, that they dream about. The end's inevitable – forget the religious take – it's evil plants, the mud, the killer bugs. There's no one left – except two actors, ripe with courage. So it ends, it all goes down, the is and ought, saying, showing – all no use at all, the guns quite impotent against the tiny things that gobble up the galaxies.

'Tina, you're a noble soul,' I say, and she says modestly, 'I've always known it, but my life has seemed to take another turn.'

The animals, 'Where can they all be going?' I ask, 'Where have they all gone?'

'They were in a hurry, that's for sure,' says Tina. 'Perhaps I'm not noble, just sociable.'

'That bird has torn your skin,' I say.

'It has rough ways, that's true ... But, considering they had no clothes, those animals kept some dignity. The people, though ...'

I see her point. If those guys some day rebel against themselves, you'd better stay indoors. I say,

'When you make revolutions, you should be measured, moderate about it. I see myself as everyman, or part of him, or maybe her. But not here, not in Amerika.'

Tina says, 'You could have followed me – that zebra...'

'No,' I say. 'They're not like riding horses, we're not made to straddle them. Besides, they've no controls, you're with the wind and fancy,' and she says,

'Don't say you're snobby about zebras,' and we still see the tails, all skittering up the road, though whether they're drawn on by hope, or driven on by hopelessness, it's hard to tell. They're going south, which is correct –

the horns and stripes, long legs outpacing short but cuddly ones. They're raising dust, where dust should not have been, and Tina says,

'The stuff, the dust they raise – toxic, for sure. There will be guys with guns and nets. I hope you make it, animals! – whatever it is you want to make,' and that is deep and true, constructing things is tough or quite impossible when mostly what you do is run.

'It's quite a mystery,' says Tina, 'even if you think the beasts are put here for our amusement – those ones there don't raise a laugh, just puzzlement.'

*

'... just skittering, all a-skeeter up the road,' I tell Gabrielle: 'Incredible. No jewels, no bells.'

'I told you,' says Gabrielle. 'That part of town is not for us,' and I say,

'Not town, a road, From somewhere on to somewhere else. Tina befriended one of them, to give it guidance.'

'Animals know what they want, is all,' says Gabrielle, briskly. 'Tina's a hostess, so of course she's friends. The trouble is,' she changes key, 'is you. You'll never shake. The tree. That's what you do with it, that's what it's for. You won't. Won't lead. Won't follow. No collateral campaign for you, ex-comrade everyman! You're the one that has no roots. I can sell, sell my birthright, if there's someone ... Tina ushers. Masha cooks.'

I add, 'Distils as well, and bottles, neatly. You all do something. The colonel's found his slot, and Fyodor...'

He's overheard. 'Roots,' he says. 'Let's find them, put the axe to them. Some bishops, apostates, went to the pyre. Neanderthals, now – there was a heap of guys in at the start, stood there, or crouched, at the founding, no one credits them,' and I say,

'Everywhere there's heaps of bones, not named, not even in the archive. Played their part. Our founding fathers, all stuffed down and burnt, just beneath the surface, global, all goes goes trundling on. A pellet in the dark. Clay.'

'A project's what we need,' says Masha, 'But first a celebration. And at the end, another too.'

'Everything is loosening up, they say. Cash, rebellion, trade. The people on the march, or saying no, at least. So, why do I feel so apprehensive?' I ask.

Masha says, 'The people. Alphabet soup.'

'We have a problem, Masha,' I say. 'The colonel. They say Fyodor's importing women – the three of you, and then there's me, the driver. Now, we know Fyodor's just rubbish – clever rubbish, though, bringing out the tenderness in us, all that ...'

Masha laughs, 'People can't be illegal, only things and deeds. Besides, a guy needs women – first, a cook, that's me. A hostess – Tina. And a manager – even a one-eyed one. There's you – someone to drive him, let him keep his hands unfettered, so's to wave ... Besides, we're assets – why'd the colonel make our lives more difficult?'

I say, 'That is his job. We must move on – but, those tunnels, no! Freedom calls – but when there are rebellions, you open up the jails, so if like us you aren't yet in one, what does freedom mean? To truck some more?'

'You've gone all cold inside,' she says. 'Let's warm you up.'

'Oh yes, I'm just a cook!' Masha laughs, jigging me about. 'I cook by colour, not by taste. That is the classic way – no sauce of rotting fish, no resin in the wine. If things go bad, well, that is nature's way, on with the feast, your eyes will draw you – taste comes usually too late to spit things out.'

We start to whirl along, past booths and lit-ups where they buy their stuff. She shouts,

'A very special cook – my ladle's longer than your arm,' and she has pinned me, flings me, and she shouts again, 'It's at the basis of it all – no, idiot, not the hunt, the kill – the basis of the song, the music, theatre, religion, everything that makes the show, the everything that ostriches don't have: – the dance! The twirling! Brings you to the centre of the whirligig, you spin, you are the clay upon the wheel, you rise right up, you're conical, you sink, a turd, then you're an empty pot, wet from your birthing – maybe you sing, maybe you pray or cry. I dance, I dance, and in the centre of the wheel, there, there is the god, at one with you in vertigo ... They say that god was all alone, and there was nothing there, no ground to hold him up, no sky above his head, no up, no down, no light, no dark. So, what could he do to while away no time, no end and no beginning, nothing, no duration ...'

We start to spin, her feet are clamped to mine – and who is pressing round, out there – Mexicans, and Indians, perhaps – the ground is red and hard, maybe we do some desecration – now, she lifts right off, she grips my hands, her hair is flailing in my face, I smell her breath like jasmine, I still stand and whirl around, and she is flying out, a horizontal, naked as a plum – she says,

'And so this lonely god, this sane and reasoning stone – the solitude! My dear – the solitude! Not to create, create the creeping fornicating things, no sins, confessions, lamentations, no lies, no massacres, no plagues, no sunset, earthquake, flood and suffocation. Just One, containing everything – or nothing – pure divinity, pure emptiness, perfection, standing there on nothing, seeing nothing, stomach empty as a dried-out gourd ...' and we are going faster now, we're circling on the clay, and spinning on ourselves and spinning on the ground, and round we go, and there is people circled here around, their eyes are closed and maybe in their heads they're circling round as well, and Masha says,

'And in this solitude, the boredom – can you imagine it?' and jasmine's all around, I draw it in, I gulp it down, she says,

'He moves. He turns. He gyres, he twirls, and as he turns, his giddiness – it grows and grows. He can't fall down – as yet there is no down. His eyes – they cannot fix upon some point, there is no sight, there is no point. He dances! – this lone, this only god, and as he goes around – into his head there comes a mass of wriggling primal things, and some with wings, and some with horns and scales, and here we are, the things with sex, we fornicate, we feast, we eat, regurgitate, and things ferment and die and crawl upon each other, and kneel and pray and shout, hallucinate, and draw upon the sand. And there are plagues, and tidal waves, and droughts, and leeches on your belly, tiny things that bore inside and grow as big as eggplants with your blood ...'

I'm hot inside, can't see my feet, my legs, and now she's pressed against me, and she weeps, she howls, she says, 'It's dying now. It's slowing, here we come, back to our solitudes, here's the clay again, and we are rooted here, goddam the vertigo, creation, all that folly, brains turned back to silt ...'

We're as we were before, just standing there, though I am warm, there is a breath of jasmine still. She says,

'And did you see? The nothing, where it starts? And ends. You saw us, saw our destiny?'

I say, 'Yes,' though I'm not sure, I really do not grasp, and what can we be doing here, the dance ... she takes me by the hand, she says, 'You just get used to it – the movement, and the awful standing still. The dance. The revelation. Disappointment too.'

Then, 'I'm quite a special kind of cook,' she says.

*

'Masha talks a lot about fornication, but I don't see much of it,' says Fyodor, glumly. 'You've picked up three of a kind, three queens fresh off the table, and don't know what to do with them. In life,' he goes on more confidently, 'there's freedom, cash, and pleasure. Those are the wild cards, and of those three, two's in the head, one in the hand – the cash, if you can land it. Maybe it only works if you have got all three. Here there's freedom, but the pleasure – that eludes. It's no good hoping that more cash turns up – that's not what you want. Back there—' and he points east, way, way east. He could have pointed west. Or north. 'Back there, I had the cash. And freedom too – but the freedom card – what good is that if you've no pleasure? Maybe some guy holds two pleasure cards...' and he's suddenly intimate. 'You see, the problem is, with these French cards, there are four suits. You're never sure if four alike is out against you. That bugger Napoleon – he brought them in, and left them there.'

I say, 'You know it all, how it works – the clubbing. Buying, selling. Here, like at home. Votes, too.'

'There's no birch trees here,' he says, and he is near a tear.

'That's quite inadequate,' I say, 'and sentimental too. Buy up that heavy gas that no one knows quite what it's for. Stability's the thing – pump! into the cellars so the houses don't fall down. Into the President's shoes, so you don't see him quiver.'

He's not quieted: 'Nah – when the Chinese come, Tina will have her friends, and Gabrielle – she'll sell them things. It's true, I have my vision – but they've got their own, and tough ones too. It may look delicate, but as for guys like me – they built a wall to keep us out. Maybe this time too – they'll stay inside. Horses and camels – that's what we were useful for. And fleecy maidens. So – what should be my cause? The southerners – they have one, and it isn't football. What is mine? Keeping people out? But they seep in like seas. What do I have? The horror. Patchouli. Cranes and griffins. I'll be overwhelmed.'

'Don't think so deep,' I say. 'The history's for amusement, better so. This here's the place for one like you: Amerika. There's casinos sprinkled round, and whores of every kind, and as for guards and soldiers – there are legions. Spying too,' and I go on, he's not convinced.

'I've done all that,' he says. 'It's true, they're angels here, with every plumage, every beak. They fly, like birds of paradise or dinosaurs or planes. But – I have lost my soul, left there, among the birch trees,' and he can't be consoled: the birch trees have all gone, I say.

'That makes it worse!' he shouts. 'Fuck Pushkin! "Farewell life in the sticks! Nobody escapes the bonfire:

If you live – you burn!" – there, that's poetry for you! Tell me if that isn't me!'

And it is, it seems to be.

*

'If we don't like it here, this unhappy place,' says Fyodor, 'we must go South. Up there – there's only Canada.'

'Oh no,' says Tina, 'Not Mexico – mescal, peyote, mystic journeys, all that crap.'

'Never mind,' says Fyodor, 'We'll go where there's no Mexicans, no Russians either.'

Gabrielle hisses, 'That'll be fine, Masha. Time for an eye for my eye. You can forget about tooth for a tooth,' and Masha shrugs, and off we go, and she says,

'But not the desert road,' and so we take the tunnel. There's guys with bundles, in the halls there's little ratty beasts and stuff alive like necklaces of sand in motion, and cops on choppers coasting up and down and taking tithes, and we run on – and then we're out!

'Fyodor, you can be planted here,' says Gabrielle and laughs. 'Our hope for a new dynasty.'

'No,' says Tina, 'he hasn't the right words – not pleasure, cash and freedom. I should say "dignity, and cash and brotherhood".'

Gabrielle says, 'We must get it right: justice, equality, and cash.'

I say, 'Now, maybe, we should all split up,' and Gabrielle takes me to one side, 'You're leaving? What will you do? And me?'

'I could be a great South American artist. A writer. Commentator. Even president. With those words ...'

She says, 'You weren't at school with the right rich kids.'

'I'd make out,' I say. 'I could pitch in with words, some on the coins, you'll find. But – we need eats, or work. My pants is quite in rags.'

She considers, 'There remains the priesthood. Here, they are specialists. Then, there's doomsaying.'

I'm irritated, and I say, 'Don't be so crass,' then, 'Is that, in your good eye, a tear? The future's terrible, I know, but it will come, and I shall go.'

'You find Masha more interesting than me?' she asks.

'Wow! Yes,' I say.

'And Tina too?'

'Not interesting. Bold. And wheedling.'

'Well,' she says, 'if you go, I'll follow on, be sure I'll spit on your drab grave.'

'I don't suppose I'll go,' I say. 'The colonel's paying Fyodor – for private information on what goes on around. Fyodor will have to make it up, or else things will be bad, so bad, for us, and meddling here...' and she stops crying, looks apprehensive once again:

'You're right to stay,' she says, though nothing binds us close, except necessity.

'I'm brighter than you guys,' I say. 'It's just I don't know much. Not the specifics.' The candle flame. All mine.

*

Here – all these white guys, black guys, everyone else, in-between guys, guys looking inside, looking outside. Being their one thing, or another. Or a mixture, their musics like flowers in a store, all bright and making their own way, inscrutable. Can't pull a meaning out.

'You're nothing special,' Gabrielle says. 'Like all men from home – hard men who cry a lot.'

Masha says, 'Cold outside. Cold inside.'

'Look!' says Gabrielle. She's built a compound. Each of us has a house, sort of. Two storeys. That way she can check us over, space us right. They're built of wicker, and of feathers.

'Snakes love to climb up wicker,' Masha says.

'We might too, but they won't hold,' I say.

'No,' says Gabrielle. 'Climbing is out. What you think I am, a homemaker? Masha, you'll sleep on the floor, where you belong. Some of these – these structures – are larger. They're my opinions, coming out.'

'The kingdom of the one-eyed queen,' says Tina.

'When they come for Fyodor, they'll find him easy here,' says Gabrielle. 'Mexico – it's where they come, from home, to find the people with the secrets.'

'If you have secrets, you're not safe,' nods Tina. 'If you don't have secrets, you're not safe.'

'It's important that the murderers – if that is what they are – know exactly where to look,' says Gabrielle, and I remember – the compound in the ice, where it all ended, all began. The keys. The vouchers. Plan for a journey, tossed away, and stolen. Well, you can start your journey any day, I guess, you're always travelling, it's just the destinations fade and modify. Companions come and go, not always fragrant, and I think – Fyodor, spy, informer, warrior – 'and cash', he says, and that is true, he is the one who's paid, so it is right he takes the risk.

What wondrous things Gabrielle has built! There's only seagull feathers in these parts, and cane – but she has dyed and plaited, feathers now of turquoise, silver. Made floors of obsidian, stairs of long-bones green with river-wash, the canes are woven in the shape of crowns – turreted, with pearls, with tiny ermine tails – here is a shape, a boar's head, there – a flashing eye: 'You put power in?' I marvel, quite bewildered.

'If you could climb the stair,' says Gabrielle, 'you'd see the sea. Look, you've each a pillow made of jade – not Masha, that is obvious. Beside each sleeping place, a lamp, so when you hear the lizards that can eat your hands, you switch it on, and they are gone. But you,' she turns to me, 'you have your candle. We all sleep alone, so it's the case that you're the one that takes some time to find the light, the match, and so you'll need to learn to cheat your destiny in quicker time.'

It's all a great invention. But – everything's invention. This one's no use. But we spend a day admiring it and touching it, and at dusk the lights come on and flash with red and green. And if the murderers come, we hope they'll seek out Fyodor – that's justice, and he's branded with the word, *adil*. But so am I. That makes it easier, for them.

'These spires. These pyres. Depressing,' Fyodor says.

'Beautifully made,' I say, 'genius behind them somewhere,' and he waves his hands and says, 'They don't need send people to cancel you – not like that Trotsky – no, death comes in an envelope. Swiss chocolates. Too bad they don't send Rusty, though – he could make a drink that stunned. He is as good as pancakes – you'd not mind if it was him that wiped you off the slate,' and I tell him Tina can mix a drink that drops you, and he says,

'They pick on one, or all – that is your luck. We sleep alone – we'd be better off in Tina's coat. If death's to be our destiny – then, what's to do? What is our point?'

I ask, 'Gangs? Arms? People? Is this the intelligence they pay you for? To check it out? The contraband?'

'Yes, that is all there is for me,' he says. 'It's trade. It goes up North. Goes to unhappy people, needing miserable ones down here to sell them useless stuff. If only ...' and he's crowds of guys with stones who change their governments. For the moment, he is hard and pure.

'Stop worrying,' I tell him. 'Greatness will come. Smell the jasmine,' but he shrugs and says,

'It comes off those stacks. It shoots up, it comes down. The smell.'

I'm silent. 'Wealth,' he says, 'It's stocking up. Not here, there's poor guys here. Scrabbling for cash, guys you'd not want sitting and joking in your truck. The rich guys and their palaces, up there,' and he gestures, 'Can't spend enough. You have to dig it up, more wealth, and burn it off, and send it on to who knows where. Rich guys – they can't eat it all and crap it out, and drive around in limousines and drink our club champagne. China now – there's room for rich guys there, and poor guys too. But it will end the same.'

'How will it end?' I ask.

'It ends. It keeps on ending. Then it starts, starts somewhere else. Until the end.'

'Of course,' he says, 'It's still worthwhile being rich. It's just necessity, you need to turn the wheel. And poverty has no attraction. No principle.'

I ask, 'Your past? Beating up on southerners?'

'Ah well,' he says, 'I'd a militia then. I was conservative. The worst thing's this being stuck, the in-between, the middle way, not rich, not poor, but serving goddam ghostly things: the power, the people, the big boss – all stuff like that.'

He makes our cash. He sings, he raps, in cabaret. It is his time of discontent, and Masha says,

'Don't bring no severed heads back here,' and my three graces sit around and think what they can do, and Gabrielle, with her bad absent eye – she peers through stones, and there's the future, all laid out and waiting, horrors, delights, and Masha's end.

*

'I found this book,' says Fyodor. 'It has no cover. It asks – "What is our Revolution, if it is not a mad rebellion in the name of the dynamic principle of life?" Here's one for Piotr: "Peasants eat in order to work, work in order to eat, and besides that, to be born, to bear, and to die." What insight! What a genius, this unsung nameless guy! It's us! It's here! "We must rebel against the peasant root, its aimlessness,"' and he goes on, inspired, and does for Pushkin, other poets too, not heard of here.

'Is that what you tell them,' I say. 'The bosses here? The people in the club? You can't throw Trotsky on them,' for I hear his echo – 'It's a sacrilege,' and Fyodor cuts in, 'There is no sacrilege, no holy. Stir them, stir them up,' and I think of Gabrielle and 'shake the tree'.

'With howls,' he says, delighted, 'I give the rap – religion, economics, leaves them cold, but when it's revolution time, they're stomping on the tables. This is the place, it's right, it's just: *adil*' – and he bares the brand, to show.

'You know, it ended bad for him. In Mexico,' I say. He shouts,

'For him, that author guy, for everyone, it all ends bad, and you and Masha too, and Gabrielle, she'll end up in a ditch. The only one who gets away is Tina, she can ride the wind – so no! you fools, you shan't feel pity for the others, horror for your end – you'll croak alone and sweating, trembling as you see the drop, the dark dark destiny. You have to let the others love the madness, let them sink and bleed, accept their fate, and into battle, sweep all away – away, away, you mobilise, you make them march – on to Persepolis or Denver, march where the hell you want! The Revolution. Here it says, "much more than candles were burned for it",' and I shout too,

'Leave my fucking candle out of it – you're quite insane. Mad monk!'

We face up to one another, and I think, 'My candle, my flicker in the gold, defend at any cost ...' and he is on me, not a plank this time – a club, it feels like basalt, there's volcanoes here – grab it and twist – we sprawl around and bite.

A spill of blood. No rancour. To the death. Then –

'The book, Fyodor,' I say. 'You must have seen the date, and all those Russian names?'

He says, 'I only read the interesting bits in books. A book is like a closet, full of things that you don't use, then you take out what serves, and lock it up again. Besides, my public, it's all Russians, most of them.'

I'm irritated, and I say, 'These guys here – they had their revolution long ago. It's their closet, like you say. And while you're quoting at them in the club – just think of me. I tidy up this place, this compound. Chase the strangers off, make sure it's their last time. Polish the obsidian. Chistka – the clean-out. That's my task.

Cleaning feathers is homework for a bird, but hard for me, a penance. Keeping things straight. There's Tina – finds a sidewalk, ushering in the guys, and after – carrying them all out. A global celebration. But – the trash she meets! And Gabrielle – she's sold this lot, this compound here, a dozen times, guys buy and come and gaze at it, they're happy now, but come the day ... it isn't ours to sell, and Gabrielle just says, "I make them happy, where's the bad? The people here are savages, they don't have notaries, and they pay in cash."'

He's silent.

'I don't trust you, none of you,' I say.

'And that's exactly right,' he says. 'It's luck, it's chance.' He declaims, '"A thought emits – rolls of the dice. Their dark spots – a constellation. Cold with oblivion, abandon. The numbers, spots on the dice – we can't see them in the dark." That's thoughts for you, unpredictable. Imagine, what a day of hustling can bring.'

I say, 'You laugh at me – thoughts, throws of the dark, the dice. It's mystification – I can see the numbers in the dark, my candle flame is quite enough. And what is more – I'm brighter than you all. It's just I don't know much. You have your thoughts, I have my principle. My mind – it's white, untrampled like a sheet of snow. Quite spotless. Immaculate.'

The dust here, and mud, it drifts, it seeps in everywhere, and while the others do their work, I clean, I purify. I see the strangers off. I say,

'It's useless, beating up on me.'

'It's not only to do with you,' says Fyodor, 'though ignorance surely has its place.'

*

'How did you kill my father?' Fyodor asks.

'Don't be childish. You were there,' I say.

'Don't lay that on us,' says Masha.

'I always fell asleep at Masha's place,' says Fyodor,

'A place you don't remember,' she concludes.

*

Masha cooks – 'No animals,' says Tina, 'My coat, those ocelots – a gift, gift from a friend. How glad they'd be, those cats, to know how useful they'd become.'

Masha laughs, and says 'The great chain of eating,' and she taps us, each one, on the head, with that long ladle, longer than my arm. She says, 'Ha! Those skull pans – each will be a vase for vegetables,' and it's true, she cooks all day, our food is red and white, 'all vegetables, gathered by night,' she says.

Vegetables for sure, with claws and paws and scales. And Tina tells us how she went out East, a hunting trip – 'I run before the guns, I cast my cloak, a poncho, shield the beasts, and they come running up for shelter, each offers me a special gift, in gratitude, for life. Those tigers, with their sabre teeth, the pairs of wolves – in wolfland there is no divorce, no separation, no fidelity to swap for cash – and dormice too, and pheasant birds with peacock crests, and dogs with wings, and eagles too, so heavy and so broad they bear you down, you lift them on your shoulders and you fall, and then they lift you up and up you go to mountains, rivers of lapis lazuli and silver filigree beneath …' and on she goes, 'and then the hunters take me, hold me back, and there was massacre of beasts. The animals – they left their gifts, and guilt and rancour too. I ride, I fly the wind, I climb and burrow, and at dawn I sound the call to wake and hide.'

We laugh: our life is built on many deaths, betrayals too, and Fyodor says,

'You'll not find all that in Pushkin. Those guys hunted without sentiment,' but revenge is in his mind. No crime in particular that is haunting him, accumulation does it all, and casts its dark on Masha's stew.

Tina's in full spate: I say, 'That big skin, then, it's a penance.'

'No, not at all,' she says, 'A penance leads to pardon – maybe to hell. My skin is punishment, I can't cast it off, it will remain, it's never less and never more.'

'But it keeps us warm,' says Masha. 'And no doubt it keeps you warm, and it attracts, gentlemen, the others, and mmmm – that smell of stew and sour, who'd not want to climb into those folds, forget and loll about. It is your Southern island, clothes you wear all over – just to conceal your sex. But sex is all over you – from naughty toes up to your chaplet, fleshy flowers. My! how I want to wriggle in, insinuate. Your skin, your sin's your fortune, it's your life and livelihood – the dead ones gone and mounted on the wall, their eyes are glass, the brain is hollowed out and fed to cats. Forget! After the something, there is nothing. Enjoy, enjoy your hunters, screw them till they scream, and take their cash and take their names, and shoot them down, if that is what you want. And no one cares – maybe there's someone knows, but that is all – behind that, there's no caring. You're in your warm skin – it is a gift, hug, fold it all around you – don't think of the dead. Don't give it back. Nor give back any gift – and when you fall, and can't fly any more, we'll put you ... There!'

She points to one of the mounds, before the cane-brake: 'And in your skin we'll bury you, your gift, your deed and good times, sins and all – there they will lie and rot. Ferment. Forgotten.'

*

Fyodor says, 'I keep a score. I don't forget,' and I think of southerners, beaten and restless, and I say, 'Some of those guys weren't bad,' and he says,

'What's badness got to do with it?' and of course he's right, where does the bad, or good, come in?

'They're not Arabs,' Tina says, 'The guys from the South.'

'Of course not,' says Gabrielle.

'Then where? Those Chechens – where'd they come from?'

'Maybe they was always there,' says Fyodor, 'Like me. I was always where I was. Beyond – there's Chinese. Besides, now, everyone is everywhere. You can't get away with things, like once. I haven't moved...' but he has. And turns back to his vegetables.

'Some people's divided into tribes,' says Gabrielle. 'That's what makes them so aggressive.'

'Maybe we should be a tribe,' says Tina. 'We're divided, and we need aggression – it's terrible out here, and severed heads is not the whole of it.'

'No,' says Fyodor, 'For tribes you need some kids. True, there's lots around. They'd join us, that's for sure. But I won't give protection to them. What can you do about kids?'

I say, 'We could be a clan. That's tight.'

Fyodor seems keen: 'Perhaps a clan would just protect the five of us. Half could take my name,' and he turns to me, 'And half could take on yours.' I do the maths, and say,

'If others join, we could even up that score. We could tattoo them – so they needn't remember names.'

'I don't see the point,' says Masha. 'And nor do you. These things are only good for settling spats – those Americans, they take revenge, and make a mess, it costs them and it doesn't pay them back. What good's revenge, if it don't satisfy?'

That seems good sense, and so we end discussion there.

*

Fyodor takes me to the club. He makes the clients strip, but leaves their shoes and boots – 'for stomping with. And for the splinters.' He keeps his clothes on, and on his head a modest peacock's crest. He jerks it up and down – 'I'm much reduced,' he says.

As he goes through the clothes, the wallets, all the stuff, he makes a note of names. Then, on the stage – it's hot in here, there is miasma from the bodies, motor oil and sauerkraut. There is applause and boos. The walls are pearl and silver, and the glitter balls are blue 'to keep the people cool' he says.

'The show, the show,' the people cry, and he begins.

He doesn't speak, he howls. He throws his muzzle in the air, and there's a long, a solo, howl. Again, again, the forest rings, the hero's challenging – and soon the crowd is howling too. They stand, they stamp. Howls for the pups, a distant choir: the hunt: the wound, despair. Courtship. A coupling.

They're wolves.

'But sociable,' he says to me. 'Once they are free, I bring them back.'

'Now, march!' he doesn't say as much, he raps a pace stick on the floor, and on the spot they march, the boots make noise like paper crumpling, the glitter balls spin round, and it's retreat, advance, attack, and victory. Their flesh is blue and silver, like a guardsman's uniform. They all look straight ahead. 'It's just a show,' he says to me.

'Freedom!' he shouts. 'Yes, yes,' they cry.

'Danger!' he shouts, 'No, no,' they cry. 'No danger, no protection, we're the best!'

He says, aside to me, 'I perk them up. It's why they pay. The bad guys, some outside, some in here,' and he waves towards the naked ones, the light, the tables, guys like quails unfeathered, skewered, 'It's all quite unpredictable. I give them hope. I strip them off. And – lots of booze,' and he shouts to them,

'Pushkin melodies?' and 'No, no,' they shout, 'Fuck Pushkin,' and they drink, they run their tabs, Tina brings ever more, and –

'You see,' says Fyodor, 'I run through the sentiments, don't even need to sing, or spin a disc.'

*

'When they are naked, then they feel free,' he says: 'That way, they can't have knives and such. And being mostly guys, they size each other up,' and he laughs: 'For me, it's too much like old times – with Tina on the door, the colonel with his eye ...'

I say, 'This here, all round – this place is terrible. We'll end up headless,' and he says,

'The thing I miss – is my political career.'

'Emperor of China? That? A wild oat, Fyodor.'

'Not exactly that,' he says. 'The colonel now, he's making discs – more Pushkin there. He's deeply into fame. And as for me – I see myself as hero of our time. That guy who fought a duel down South, a Pushkinite. He lost. I'll win. Then – off with the grey men, godfather cops! I'd bring some colour in,' and he waves his peacock crest.

I say, 'You'd cut me in? You trust me, Fyodor?'

He's silent for a while, then, 'It's not the cash. The noise of being – that's the thing. You shout, you stamp, and – did you know, the sound goes on forever, it's like a rocket, boundless, round and round the galaxies, into other universes, infinity of time and space – but not infinity like you can't hear or see, it's with you like the mermaid in your ear. It's waves, undying swash of sea, a shout that hangs like jasmine flowers, that's in your sleep, your nose, your tongue. The shout of history, my friend, that terrifies or takes your clothes, and makes you howl and stamp ...' and Tina hears and rushes in and says,

'You're starting it again, the Revolution,' – the world, we feel it shake, and heavy gas is useless now, the street is full of free and naked guys, though Fyodor has all their names. And Tina shouts,

'It's time to hunt the hunters down!' and she is like Diana, draped, it is magnificent – and Fyodor rears up, he shouts in turn, 'Hey guys! We're closing now, and time to get your clothes,' and so they do.

I say, 'Your philosophy, Fyodor, it's quite transparent.'

'No sex, all sex,' he says. 'No need to hire a band. No Napoleon in view, no big ending, just the little ones. Reconciliations, and revenge. We're orphans of the revolution, my friend, – not Tina, she's too young to be an orphan,' and Tina interrupts,

'There's always been them – revolutions, and one day there'll be an end to cops and spies. A sidewalk and a club – that's all you need,' and Fyodor is angry, says he can't stand cynics, says, 'You see – it all returns to me, back to my triumphant scene, where there's no media, no mediation. Just the naked, having their good time. Me at their heads.'

'You're a great benefactor,' I say, flattering. 'Suffer for the people, but don't tell. That's the spirit!'

'Suffer? Rubbish!' says Masha: 'The only tale that's plausible in history – is Onegin. It all starts with Larina, bottling. Anything without a cook to start – the characters all will die. Or eat each other. Adverbs and cooks, that's what you need to make a story go. You leave the people out – there is no room. You need a duel, of course – Fyodor and you, maybe. And one of you cast down, the other shot.'

'Masha,' I say. 'I lost that duel a while ago. A sausage, from behind. Humiliation. Ridiculous. Besides, we're all professionals, warriors, like when we slept, all rolled up and battle-ready, like a bunch of radishes – in Tina's coat. All sex, no sex. It's true, it's not a story.'

'We'll all go back,' says Masha, weeping – her memories bring it on herself, the longing. She turns to me. 'You could live again, back in the cold. To flee – what had you done?'

'What we all do there, to keep alive. So now you know, I can't go back. The price is much too high,' but I have no regrets, just – where we are is severed heads and worse.

*

'You don't need to be a mystic,' Masha says. 'To see right into your head, right through it. That plank, the mortadella – opens it up. Like everyone with a wound. The stick, the carrot – pain's the same. Gabrielle's eye – she can't see out, you can see in.'

I say, 'Revenge is out – we're precarious here, why bother with old scores? Gabrielle may hate you, but it's thought, not deed. Look, the armed men are all around. Still. Pistols, machetes! If only what we had was precious – some idea, could save us, or condemn. We could bargain, but these guys – they don't want bargains. Just circling round. It's not their fault – addiction, it's a powerful discourse, it's always kept us stuck together. Like your cooking, Masha. Where would you be – where would I be without ...' I don't go on, I think of food, ideas. I run my hands all over her, and she stands quiet and still. It's jasmine on the bough, and after a long while I say ... 'without you?'

Is there a tear? An answer to the question, unasked, and she stands still as if she's answering, then she says,

'Don't delude yourself. It's not you, not about you. You're a flake.'

'Tell me your secrets, Masha,' I say.

'I don't have any. They're yours, all of you, seen all around, you here, the guys behind those mounds. Secrets – they're not mine, and not exclusive. I observe, and see them all.'

*

Gabrielle says to me, 'I spy you – up against that Masha, like a goat scratching against a pole. It won't do any good, to either,' and I say,

'Those guys are circling round again. Fyodor should sort them out. They used to come to trade behind the club. But now they're here.'

'There's always lots of pasts involved,' says Masha. 'There always are. They're chains. Some modern, and some ancient. All this stability, the gas beneath – it's often quite a pain,' and on she goes, and we agree, some pasts go on for centuries, others fly and pass like maybugs – in the end they're fossils piling up, they seem inert, but when you try to make a choice – some are quite seductive, most are dust and hairs – they slip and slide like potter's clay. We nod and yawn, it doesn't quite connect. We, here, have no stability, the things just happen, we don't have much past. The present and the future – they appear quite squalid, but we welcome them each day, they are the dawn, fingers aglow, like rosebuds, or it may be blood. The gods are newly at their post and greet you with a smile, and even giggle as you rise. On with the burdens, the yoke, and off you go ...

Here's Fyodor, he's running, and he shouts, he screams, 'Retreat, retreat! Take up your cash and armaments – and run!' And he is running, a leaf before the wind, the rain, and there are guys all round. It doesn't matter who they are or what they represent, it's time to run, and that is all.

'Where do we go?' asks Tina as she runs, a scamper like those animals ...

'Money! my money! – it lies, quiet and earthy, in a mound,' says Gabrielle, and she gestures emptily towards the stand of canes – 'And palaces! My palaces!'

I think, 'My cleaning!' but we can't take that either, it's heavier than palaces, being procedure, a state, a concrete abstract, and I laugh: 'Where now?'

'Quick!' says Fyodor. 'A problem of supply, now it's arisen, here it is, with acid breath. Talons of steel. Another country – quick!'

We run around like horses tethered, no time, nor will, to say goodbye to those we love and those we hate. Then, Tina ...

... look! She spreads her coat, her dappled skin. There's room for all. It will protect. Sure, we don't become invisible, or fly, but now we pass under another sign. We are the jaguar, the largest ever, in the kingdom of the beasts.

We scuttle off. We can't go back.

'Those weren't the murderers that come for Fyodor,' says Masha. 'Those ones are quite a different crew.'

*

'The guy that poled us over the water – he charged us, but going back is free,' says Gabrielle: 'I told him, I'd no intention of dying here.'

'This seems quite a basic kind of place,' says Fyodor.

'I don't feel like building palaces for you guys here,' says Gabrielle: 'I want my free ride back.'

We're quite demoralised – 'And everything was taking shape,' says Fyodor.

'Freedom and dignity – the path, bright before us,' I say: 'Then, Tina was our protection – to be a saint, you don't need a religion – that would diminish it,' and Tina says,

'Not my saintliness – my coat protected you. I'm off – there must be bars –' and she waves her hand towards the high buildings far away, 'with sidewalks for the guys, and work for me. But I shall leave my coat – it will be your banner, tattered like the Turcomans': "white sheep", "black sheep". But this is ocelot, the largest you will ever see.'

We raise it on a stick.

*

'Tina runs off because she hates routine,' says Fyodor sagely. 'Runs off to find another – routine, but with a different boss. For her kind of freedom, she needs wings: not paws, another animal to ride.'

'She leaves her emblem,' I say, pointing to her skin, 'It's bold, and Southern too.'

'No bigots here,' says Fyodor primly. 'Now, we need a fortress and some guards. A star, five points – that's the surest kind of shape to fortify a place – you sally out, then run back in.'

I'm not so sure, but he's convinced. There's no one round about, and we have nothing – but the danger, yes, that's always with us.

'There's nothing to report,' says Fyodor. 'Nothing to spy on – though of course there is each other. We shall make that do, and leave the Colonel sing his songs.'

*

'We used to think food was a metaphor for sex,' says Masha, 'but now it seems it's not: it is for hitting. Those drugs they use back there – is kind of food, and guns is what you use to sharpen up the appetite. Then there's the women, slaves – it's all a trade. It's like those tribes, you've heard of them, women and salt, at least some powdery stuff. It all rotates. What could you expect, the globe is like that too, and round and round it goes, its pustules and its wrinkles ... What I want, is go back to my hut, the chickens, conjure up some birch trees, just the memory's enough,' and Gabrielle says that's what peasants want, and trade is something else. She says,

'Pushkin was against the peasant, wanted a world of gentlemen and duels and all that stuff. Like me – I want some rich and powerful guy that I can cleave to,' and here she nudges me, but I cleave closer to my candle flame, a wonder that it can illuminate us all, and then she says there's lots of countries waiting for a guy like me, and leaders never take exams, they just do it, lead – and when they've dropped their friends, there's always plenty more. and Fyodor shouts out,

'I'm not a gentleman,' and bares his rump, there is the just, *adil*, he says there's justice in those severed heads, and Masha says,

'The Colonel was no gentleman, so how come he liked Pushkin?'

'That was his cover,' Fyodor says, 'And he kept the score in severed heads.'

*

'Things were going well,' says Fyodor. 'So now they must go better still. No one knows where we are. And nor do we.'

Masha says, 'These snaily things – I'll add some colour, and they'll stew up fine, and look like that green ferny stuff, those fiddleheads. Perhaps.'

Fyodor goes on, ‘We can’t go back up North,’ he says. ‘So maybe I should back the South? Those guys: simple and loyal. It’s true they haven’t learned to march in step, but they are keen. No football. On the banner we can add a lion and sunface. Then – sacrifice. For years – we must all be prepared,’ he turns to me, ‘You’re ready for it?’

I say, ‘Yes, everything, it’s all about some sacrifice. That’s life, you win, you lose, and in the end...’

‘The thing to do,’ says Fyodor, ‘is to forget the end, and concentrate on victory. Constructively to use tradition ...’ and on he goes, he’s at the head – a band, a ministry, a speech – his men, perhaps his women too, exchanging views, deferring to the wise.

‘Why not?’ says Gabrielle. ‘The world is full of people you have never heard of – rising up and leading guys. There’s lots of military roads around, you find the right one, and you persevere.’

She doesn’t say these guys will shake the tree, maybe they won’t, but they have left their desks, their fields, their shacks, they look for trees to shake. She says,

‘You don’t need be the soldier, but the guy that makes him march.’

*

Next day, two guys arrive.

One says, ‘That creepy guy who poles the boat, what did he charge you guys?’

'It must depend. You're from the Colonel, you both have that air,' and one says,

'We don't know colonels,' and the other almost silently intones, 'faith and inspiration, and life and tears and love,' and repeats, 'Nah, colonels is out, they're not your gentlemen', and the other takes it up: 'The pains of love are dear to me, so let me die – but let me die loving,' and Masha hears him and she says,

'That's some crap thought,' and they both say,

'We're Fyodor's friends – where does the bastard hide?'

I think a while, a little while, I calculate and say, 'He must be over on that ridge. He'll be at his practising. It's our next step, the next time, get it right, our Revolution. That is his mission, though it must be said, it's one step forward, two steps back,' and laugh, and they laugh too.

*

Now Masha pulls my arm, and says, 'You haven't learnt a thing – you gobbled down my gherkins and my chanterelles, they didn't shake you! Everything you've thought of, all those nights, on that obsidian floor, and running with the animals, and running from the guys with guns – it didn't mean a thing to you. Now you've betrayed him – our Fyodor.'

I say, 'Masha, that past was lie and fun, it didn't mean a thing. Those guys will seek out Fyodor – who knows what end they'll make for him? He was an artist, now perhaps he'll be a martyr to the cause, although it's true the cause is always changing and the guys around are rising up and falling back, and need a hand to set them straight, that's freedom, where it takes them, who can tell, it's in the logic of the thing – you can't foretell...'

Gabrielle has given them directions, off they go, and I am proud to give poor Fyodor a hand with destiny, and up those two guys go, over the ridge ... I think of the blow that Fyodor gave me, and though I'm not vindictive – still, you don't forget, and memory's the only thing that makes us sure that we're alive.

'It's destiny for sure,' says Gabrielle, and turns to me, 'At last, it's your chance to be a leader, make your piece of history, I'm so proud ...' and Masha says,

'Be sure they'll come for you as well, you creeps,' and so she too has sealed her destiny – she isn't loyal, as you must be when you are one of three. It's true, that Gabrielle looks better when she sleeps – awake, she is a dried-out root – but we can take a pace or two together down the path, and we shall seek out Tina's bar, Tina can steal us food, as Masha won't be there to cook for us.

So, I plan the future, and those two guys, that say they're friends of Fyodor, we don't see them again.

We don't see Fyodor again, we don't expect to. So, we have a wake, to reassure us that if things went bad for him, he'll know there was remembrance here.

*

'You know what this is?' Masha asks – she twirls it round her head. 'I found it in the road, in our last place.'

'Masha – I must confess,' I say, 'I am a Southerner. and Gabrielle is too. And this – this is a bola, and you use it to lassoo,' and Masha interrupts, 'An ostrich, round its neck. It will drop down,' and Gabrielle too interrupts, 'Yes, it would. It surely would.'

We think of Tina's ostrich, and of Tina too. Ushering. And eking out in ways ...

'You bastards,' Masha says. 'You let them do for Fyodor, and he was all repentance and potential – see how he ditched the football, prejudice, enthusiasm – on with the statesmanship and wisdom. Yes, it was a true transformation – but now, you two, I'll have a guess at what your futures are and, since this is a wake, I'll celebrate. But not too loud.'

I ask, 'What do you see for me? You see me driving tumbrils,' and I laugh. She doesn't laugh, she says,

'I see you organising things. On the cellar steps your guys, and booting down the other guys, down, down they go all in a heap. Some shots. And home to lunch.'

She whirls the bola, and it takes us both, Gabrielle and me, and parcels us. It's tight about our necks, we're closer than we've been before – our breath, it's like a twist of smoke that struggles through a keyhole.

The bola binds us like two ostriches. I see that I can look up Gabrielle's nose – I must be a shortie – and I look up, through her long and tortuous nose, past the mechanism of the eyes, and there it is, her skullpan, smooth and celadon.

It's not here, the moment when I say, 'I love your skull,' – perhaps it never comes.

We're suffocating in each others' skin, hers as white as buffalo cheese, and Masha twitches on the rope, there is no room to breathe, the dream cuts in – here they come, the palaces that Gabrielle builds – there's guys with hods that fly around like dragonflies and plait the straw, and they don't need a scaffolding: there are no doors, it seems there's strobes from somewhere, red and green like peacock's tails ... and who could live in them, those palaces, those wicker bowers?

'Now,' shouts Masha. 'Prepare for the erotic scene, the last before you both go down, you pair of paranoids, traitors to us all, you would-be chieftains, vain, puffed-up –' and it is true, and as we fade and pale away, here comes the hanged-man syndrome, and I think of mandrakes – and the shame, down there's the crowd a-buzz, a sea whipped-up – and all my dreams of training guys and making them be free – it wisps away, and there is Gabrielle, she gasps, she whispers, 'Love, love and abandon', but we're caught in the lassoo, it's tighter, stricter, and we yield to it.

Afterwards, we lie there on the sand. We see the ridge, where Fyodor ... The scene is blue and breezy, looks like Holland, centuries ago, with boat-shaped clouds, the air – brass filings in our nose. It's silent as a painting, water and sky are motionless, we are alone and free, the bola round our necks unwinds.

Masha leaves, and says, 'It's history, you know I cannot intervene and turn it other ways. You bastards will go on to do what all the other bastards do.'

It seems inadequate to call us that, the world is open for me, my design: and Masha walks away.

*

Gabrielle is there – her bottle makes a gash in Masha's head – who keeps right on, she doesn't flinch or turn or run, and scores are settled, in a way, and Gabrielle would strike again, but she is weak. She leans against me, and I think, 'we're bound together'. Now she sleeps, and Masha's far away, she's walking North, the safety of her hut, the goodness under oil, and under vinegar.

'Gabrielle, we'll have more friends,' I say.

I wish that Masha'd taken me and whirled me round again, but – 'Did you see the white light, like they say?' asks Gabrielle. I say,

'I saw the flame, the candle flame, just like I always do.'

Behind, there's that black wall.

Perhaps we'll meet up with Rusty. He could be a friend. All Southerners, together. Now, there's Gabrielle.

*

I set out on my journey.

# Free at Last

'Life's a damn' queer business,' Garcia said.
André Malraux, *Days of Hope* (*L'Espoir*, 1938)

'CATCH ME that fish!' she cries. The waiter hunts it wildly with a net, then: 'No, no, leave it be. Why should it suffer for me?'

The tank calms down. This shacky eats-place ... too close by the wood. I hear the sliced up trees moan raw beneath our feet – a front line gone down, a noble worn-through landscape shuffled, obscured, now planks.

I tell her, 'You needn't suffer – yes, this is the end, an end, but nothing's lost. Experience – it's still all yours. Reflect!'

I think – there is a quest. But there is no path, no light that guides you'd want to follow.

She says, 'You wander, that way you'll end up – who knows where? All your friends cast off, now me! Where does it go? Is it a joke – love's ruins? You dig and dig, and there is no one, just scraps and broken stuff, heads probably, and stories wild, made up about it all.'

Best to keep quiet – then, 'It's not the trees you hear,' she says, 'They grow tall to be cut down, besides, it must be birds you hear – they trill. Fuck the birds.'

'Are you sad we're going separate ways?' I ask. 'Or is it just the grind of time assails? The moving on they say is good for you?'

'Two pieces, fretted out, that don't quite fit,' she says. I think she'd like to weep. The waiter wants to end his shift, he says, 'You can cry as well outside.'

'No,' I say to her, 'it's not about the pieces fitting side by side, or not. It is the picture they compose.'

In the movie, we should leave separately. Here and now, they want to lock the door. I say, 'This eatery – it's too close to the trees.'

The waiter says, 'You tell that to the trees. Besides, you two, you don't consume,' he pushes, and we're out.

She tells me, 'When you're old, your space will all be filled with screaming people, mouths like plague pits – who'll see to you then?'

I say, 'Gabrielle, I couldn't care ... and here you are, they are, already. Screaming,' and I add, 'Just let me dump you, delicately – stride off. Not through this wood, it's too provisional. A good exit, not pursued, is what I ask. I'm going where there's angry people ...'

'There's one angry here,' she says, 'and friends – where are they? My money too?'

I say, 'Friends? Some up, some down, there's always more in waiting. Your cash? Think of me as your banker – you're in luck, you get some back.' I give her a roll of notes, the little ones on the inside hiding ...

'The path,' she insists. 'You made it – look! There it lies, behind. You can't go back, of course – see how it shines – and onward – nothing.'

It shines, yes, but not illuminates. The next step always must be made in darkness. I say, 'No mixed emotions, now – straight on, avoid confusion. Remember – all those living statues, covered in gold paint. It sets. Now they're our resource, they're in a vault somewhere, pure metal. That's the lesson – what happens if you're standing still. You land in rich man's jail, and no one wants you.'

At last, that's over. Now, to sort out my head –

You make your mind a space. Quite huge and flat. A place d'armes, a champ de Mars. Pave it, if you like, with sandy stones, though I prefer the greyish-green, old mud, the travertine with fossils. Discrete, in corners, there's your former lives – a family, if you had one, old friends too. You stack them far away, perspective makes them tinier still ... A statue? On a plinth, with wheels. You want some traffic? – some classic cars, a horse, and cuirassiers. Be careful not to fill it up, the space. A corner well laid out – that's your memory, a vegetable plot in clumps and rows – not cabbages but names, of kings and movie stars, a row of clubs and bars once visited. Not radishes, but roots. Mathematics. The many, just names – you can't have met them. This is just your memory, dead laid out – potatoes. Here's the Wyoming kale, the matrioska onions, gone to seed, the purple-crested broccoli ... There's your beliefs, all nicely mounded up against the frost, and crisp, last for a summer. Weeds – so, rip them out. What's left? – there's maybe pepper plants, as hot as hellfire. Throw them in the soup.

The memory space, the garden, to remember, to store up, so you can forget. You need someone to light it up – not Gabrielle. Now, new guys can scurry in and fill the space, it's huge: and run and run, and wave their banners, handkerchiefs, their hands – and somewhere you are here as well – you can wave back. But when the movement's over, the guys cleared off – there it is, the space, the square, the empty plain. It's yours again, like now.

*

The lady shows me a dank room, a wedge of wall between the walls of other places which are dry, more decent. There's piles of books, made into primal tables by the damp, glued into shape by one another. She says,

'The guy, old Franco, he who stole the stuff and left it here, he won't cause you harm. He's only here in daytime – so, I'll chase him off: and for cash – the place is yours.'

The guy that steals the books – I see him running up and down the streets, pursued. He says,

'I have a place beneath some stairs, but in the day they cook the onions. It's a restaurant, quite suffocating, so by day I study here.' I say,

'I shan't trouble you,' but of course, that's exactly what I shall, and have him take the goddam mouldied books away, unstick them somehow, and he says,

'This little space – I've made it mine, and filled it full with civilisations – some went on for centuries, and no one cared that people's life was tough and short. The gods! Those bastards! The one they say was flayed! The spring comes anyway, without the human sacrifice and all the crap of taking off your skin and being strangled or some such, all that, the trumpets, turquoise serpents, knives,' and on he goes, 'This little space – I've made it full of wheatfields, tiny windows in mud palaces, verandas for the veiled; those birds that fish, the guys that pound the dead men's bones to make them fit in pots of porphyry ...'

I say, 'I too have made a space inside. and lay them all to rest, the friends, the childish things, to remember, to forget,' and he shouts and shakes me,

'No, no, you fool! That's just your petty stuff. I mean – whole civilisations, no one has ever counted them, their years, their dead, their massacres – and down they went, their people lost their hope, their path ... And now, you fool, the civilisations rise and fall, and no one sees or cries, we wander round, our eyes are white and blank –

here comes another one! – a civilisation that lasts a year or two, and makes its orphans, makes some gods. Those bastards! Then it sinks away, and no one cares ...'

I grasp him by the throat. He's old, and he smells bad, though I smell worse. The onion is the oldest root that grows in gardens of the mind; I think of mine, in rows, they're wilting – minds and memories don't irrigate. I say,

'Old Franco, forget the crap of civilisations, and all that. I want this room, and if it's on the street you go, it is God's will,' and he plays pitiful, he says,

'Young guys like you, you need your space. Now, there's this institute, you just walk in and take a room, and say you study there, and when the staff has all gone home, you just camp down – there's stuff to drink at every hour, and no one bothers you. You even get to go with them – an expedition ...' and I shout,

'No, no, no expeditions – I have seen them all, they look for skulls and swords and gold, they desecrate and speculate, and then they sell the lot. No, no, it's unworthy, and some other sorts is worse – movies: stuffed with sacrifice and sex, they're made for afternoon TV, "here come the primitives, the spaced out fools on magic drinks, they mutilate themselves for cash, they sell their children ..." Yes, but the colours, yes!'

But – Franco is right, why settle for this squalid place when palaces are empty, and for free?

'I'll tell you secrets, if you'll let me be,' says Franco. 'Always leave, never be left, that's one. Behave as if you've lots of cash, people can't wait to give you more. If you must – go with a bang, like the song says. If possible, lots of bangs. Excess makes its mark, modesty falls beneath the foot. If you play the madman, you'll escape the punishments – if you play the fool, you won't. Make – if you can – a loud discordant noise: people will wait to see the fragments gathered up, resolved into a harmony.'

I say, 'And is that all? Those aren't secrets, secrets are specific.'

He says, 'Here's one, then, that lets me stay and moulder with these books. You go and see this guy – he'll see you straight, no expeditions, no oaths, no loyalty, and no tests. Persuades you with his resonance, disposes of real space, not those memory plots, the old-time brain space that the Jesuits sell.'

I trust him, and I say, 'It's all to put some order ...' and he laughs, and says,

'Without water, even onions die,' and that is true – aloes and oleanders, they remain, but all the rest is halms. I say,

'It's rather good, when you forget, it's halfway over; no one sees ...' and he says,

'Yes, that's another of my secrets. My, you're learning fast.'

I trust him, and I go and see his guy. He is on the phone – I've seen so many like him, one foot in heaven, one hand holding on to Satan's tail. I hear,

'No, I'm not interested in your money I'm interested exclusively in mine. And – you won't change, but everything around will change. For centuries, the bosses grumbled that the other guys below were living off them – now, we must live off each other,' and he turns to me, and says,

'There is no path, no forward, and your past is unreliable. You're stuck inside your skin – but for a while, you have the use of spaces in your mind. Mind – ah yes, a wonderful thing, kaleidoscope. It doesn't cost a cent, but in the end, you have to hand it in, and on the tip it goes, all crumpled up. Then the earth goes on it, then the gulls. Not to mention friendly writhing things.'

I wait: 'My job?'

'This is the task,' he says – 'Just to collect my mail. You'll see it goes to Mister Marlin, and comes from – but since you're curious about names, I'll finesse you – it goes from genius to genius. There's some mystery there, I rather breed it, mystery, though in the end it's ignorance. The trouble is, we don't quite know what happens, so we don't know if we're experiencing things again. Pictures, frames – they don't fit together.'

'Do you get much mail?' I ask.

'Hardly any,' he says, 'But it's still your job to check.'

'And in return?' I ask.

'I'd spare you all these details, commonplaces, the bargaining – but there's exchange for everything, and return – for nothing. Unless,' he pauses, 'You can extort it.'

'Hmmmm,' I think. 'Suppose the board and lodging that I get for checking on the mail – is just some spaces in our heads – it may be mine, it may be his. That way, you can't stretch out, or ask in guests, or even change the sheets.'

'If sheets you have,' says Marlin, 'that's not guaranteed.'

There's fussy music playing here, turned up loud. Sometimes it flattens guys against the walls. The boss's girl – well, what a fool he'd be if she weren't beautiful.

'You must be the boss's girl,' I say, an effort to be intimate, and she just says,

'You start them off, these global corps, they bear a name – like Marlin. On they roll, a little planet – we cling on.'

'I'll just collect the mail,' I say. 'There's almost none.'

She laughs and says, 'Maybe you should have asked a little more. There's hardly any mail, but you will find it comes all round – to Ulan Bator and to Senegal, White River and South Georgia too. You ride through wars and famines – if a place has changed its name or loyalty, you must visit old and new. My dear, we shan't see you for years – for ever: we'll not know if you are dead, deserted, joined some partisans and live in caves, or are a worshipper of seas and surf the silver waves.' On she goes, and now I see – how dangerous it is to ask for work.

She says, 'I'm Candy. If you wish, I'll write to you.'

'Candy, you can leave us now. You've heard it all before,' says Marlin, but she cuddles up to him and grins at me. He says,

'A while ago, I saw the title on a shelf: *Production of Commodities by Means of Commodities*. The book made no sense to me – but the title, yes! Things reproducing things. Everything that is, reproducing everything else. The book – produces books. Civilisations – yes, they produce the books, you've seen old Franco's catacomb, but that's a different thing. Women produce women. Feelings ... but you grasp the drift. Love – love. Hatred – hatred. War ... and so on.'

He waits for glimmers in my face, and then goes on, 'You grasp all this – and so, you rule the world. The problem is – it's not enough. You keep your tab on people, know about them in your depth. Then you can fire them, or promote them, they are pleased or not – it's up to them, and up to you. It's like you learn at school – the animals make animals, parents in due time make parents, life makes death. And then – so what?'

'It's a lot, though, even so,' I say. He presses on.

'That's quite banal,' he says: 'The interest comes if people have a path, and look for meaning – the picture lying beneath the paint, the word beneath the print ...' and Candy interrupts, and says,

'No, that's not right. You've got it wrong way round again,' and Marlin says, 'Fuck off. I just explain things to this stupid guy in terms he understands.'

I say, 'Then there's a path? You think?'

'Who knows,' he says, 'who cares. It's really quite unlikely. It's the intricacy that counts – that's why the people take to arms and turn things upside down, and try to knock me off, and Candy too,' and on he goes, – 'That guy you cheated out his space,' he says, 'old Franco – he was one who had a path, the fool.'

There is a pause, and then he says, 'He had your job as well,' and Candy says,

'Don't think of cheating us – you have to make the round,' and Marlin says,

'From every place you have to send a postcard with your thumbprint – shows you've checked, and since I see you're thinking how to cheat on that – often I go and wait for you. There's no way out.'

We stand around – he's tall and thin, so thin I wonder if his body is his own. He says, 'The thing is – indeterminacy. That's how we grow, invent, and then transcend. In the beginning there was nothing, then a thing created all the other things, and on it goes. The guys who think they know, who have fixed stars and compass points – it's those will take up guns, defending errors, bigotry. They're the ones we must resist.'

I say, 'And how?'

'With guns, of course,' he says. 'When that's the point.'

'I'll take him round the plant,' says Candy, and I wonder if she means some tree, but no. He nods, he says, 'You, guy, dare cast your cold eye on Candy, and I'll pop it with a fork.'

He waves us off, and Candy says, 'He only talks about his luck, his cash, the genius that makes the luck and cash, and now has fluttered off. He hates things fixed – except for me – he's sure I'm his for life,' and so we climb a mound, she holds my arm and chatters in my ear about the sheds below, and access roads, she smells of jasmine, and I hold her close, my mouth – it tastes of onions, I am sure, but so it goes, and we recline to watch the scene, it's strange there are no birds, no grass, but I am hooked on Candy, and she says,

'The things – they reproduce themselves down there,' she points, there's guys on chairs with shotguns by the sheds. 'It's eventualities, you see,' she says, 'It's all quite indeterminate, so Marlin feels he's justified, and here we reproduce – quite indiscriminately – things that will resist the heat, the cold, disasters, overcrowding – all that stuff. Our future. What can survive. End of the world – that too.'

'You mean – prepare for the cataclysms – thick skins and body hair, and paddled feet and sticky hands?'

'That kind of stuff,' she says, 'but more. Those guys with guns – we breed bacteria, in the night they grow quite feisty. When they know they're just a power source, up through the roof they try to go – and we can't let them loose,' and I believe her, thinking of the living statues, silver, gold, how the skin is hardened all the way inside. I say,

'I bet you've dragons too, and snakes of steel.'

'Yes, yes,' she cries, 'All that, and lovers too, who let you buy the clothes you like, lovers – you hang them in the closet, out the way, they can even make the bed, they're almost natural – oh yes, our Marlin has the common touch. Forget the fetishism of commodities – our commodities are fetishes. There to enjoy,' and I say,

'It makes you want another even as you wear one out,' and she says yes, that is a slogan that may well survive the globe, and maybe put it in a spaceship, send it off, that's indeterminacy and freedom too, and I can see that taking Candy for myself and doing Marlin down and keeping both my eyes, my job as well – it's quite a task, a mission too.

She says, 'Some guys with missions really make him hurt,' and then her phone goes, and she says, 'That is my brother, we took drugs last night,' and a voice shouts, 'Help me, help me, I don't know where I am...'

She says, 'Are there trains?'

'Yes, yes,' the voice exclaims.

'Then you're at the station,' Candy says.

'Where's the station?' asks the guy.

She turns him off, we kiss some more, and I've some questions of my own, but leave them be.

'Marlin's a big fish, you know,' she says. 'Big fish tell tales,' and I say,

'Laughing at me's cheap – it's you that might tell tales, besides.'

'Don't think it means a thing – the kissing and all that,' she says.

I say, 'What could it mean? It's just more indeterminacy.' She says,

'And don't think you've some virtue: for me, it's last night talking.' I tell her,

'It's nothing, if it's not repeated – then it's nothing. And on and so.'

The guy she calls her brother – on the phone. 'Just tell him he is where he is,' I say. 'No fixed points, no landmarks.'

Candy says, 'I don't know why he's troubled – location's just a minor thing.'

*

Marlin's on his phone – 'Yes, everything makes everything else. And everything has a price, and labour doesn't enter. Yes – everything can quite become another thing – indeed, it must, the concrete into abstract, works into goodness – and the other way around. Thought into neurons, passion into glands ...' and on he goes.

Candy says, 'It's quite profound, I think,' and we wait, and contemplate indeterminate things, and how that may include the fixed as well. Like Candy. And I say,

'I don't quite understand,' and she repeats, 'It's luck and money – more than he can spend, the more he spends, the more comes in. He's into paint, and little telephones and messages and copyright, old porno movies, particles and doctorates, it has no end. Except one thing – his genius has flown away. Now, it's only cash and rhetoric,' and she looks fondly at Marlin, then she shouts again – her brother, so she says, and 'How the fuck do I know where you are, if you don't know,' and I recall – before this Candy, all those other fruits that bobbed along and promised nothing, and I made them part of quests and missions, we were bored, they went away and sent me postcards, and I say,

'You know, I've something on me that is fixed and cannot change. It's branded on me – "justice". I must be just to do it, or believe in it, yet when I'm just – the justice flows away, it isn't me, my quality, at all, but something other guys will bow their heads to have, even the guilty ones,' and Candy says,

'I hope you'll do some awful things, or else you won't fit in. Don't tell Marlin you've a fixed thing on your flesh. Say it is mortality, if you must, then he'll understand.'

*

I ponder this, and later overhear, 'Just let him have some sugar, Candy – not too much, enough to tie him in and do his job until we cast him off.' It's Marlin. Candy says,

'He's like plasticine, but I fear he has a brand, tattoo – something like that, his generation all have tried to write a sign upon their skin that ties them down upon the globe, now it begins to tilt and gyre. Poor things, each wants a special sign that tells them who they are and where they are – but now the signs are all the same, what difference does it make, if you are you and somewhere too?' and Marlin says,

'Yes, yes, that's right – dear Candy, one and only acolyte,' and on he goes with flattery and plots, and now I hear the sound, a ground bass from the sheds, bacteria as big as iguanas, climbing everywhere, their proto-limbs are indigo, elastic – and they hum along, no melody that's recognisable. Just indeterminate.

*

I ask Candy, 'Why's Marlin obsessed about his mail? Why does he chase it everywhere?'

'Hungary used to be full of writers, but none of them was Hungarian. It bothers him,' she says.

'I quite see that, but ...'

'It's him not wanting to miss an idea – not having any of his own, not now, he wants to catch them wherever they alight, he recognises spots, the wings – they are his butterflies.'

'So,' I say. 'My crap job's so important? You know – I want to take it over, all of it – the Corp. You too, if you're included – not your brother though, the guy – we don't know where he is, his loyalties; being an underground is his best gift ...'

'You've got a woman,' she says, 'and a trucking skill.'

'You can't truck to South Georgia. And the woman – well, you want someone to have a project for you, then you see it's all for her, and so you cast them off, and you're alone, you always are, and you survive, and others are cast down in turn, and maybe they find mystery though it's improbable, and Marlin's right, it's best to bet on the uncertain, you don't win, nor do you lose—'

'He's so much cash,' she interrupts, 'it comes in like the tide each day, and he must spend it – on the unforeseen: that way it disappears, and in comes more, it goes on handouts, charities, on buying castles, statues made of gold and made of plexiglass, on peace and war, on famines, on obesity, on diets, floods and dams, music and silence, hospitals and jails. On me too – to keep an eye on you.'

'Aha!' hopefully I say, 'you get his cash? Old Franco worked for him, and now he's destitute.'

'My money is ephemeral,' she says, 'and so I spend it on ephemera – that is a motto of the house, the dynasty. Old Franco cheated on his rounds. The punishment – is always just. Comes from the top. You ought to know.'

*

I say to Marlin, 'So, you're Hungarian?'

'Whoever told you that?' he asks. 'My parents weren't. I am. Yes.'

We feel awkward, he less than me, perhaps.

Employees – you can hear a background mousy scurry as they move about behind the walls, the hangings, portraits – all false, I imagine. Wainscotting. He says,

'It's more democratic, to have the guys behind. That way you can't look down on them. No one puts on airs. For all you know, they could be naked.'

We stare out the windows, high and sealed.

He says, 'Those sheds down there, where we prepare for best, and mostly worst – they look industrial, just asbestos roofs, titanium doors, to keep the things inside. But – they're a special kind. It's all tooled silver up above, and finest bronze elsewhere. You know, we guys – the former, now the burned-out, geniuses – we have more power than Genghiz, though we're brighter and more modest too. Childless as well – it's best. That guy, the military Mongol – he didn't grasp. The future he laid down was wholly fragmentation, the splitting up of everything. Terminal cooling, squabbles, grandeur overstrained. All that. Now, it isn't just the messages that common people send around – at twice the speed of Puck – remember him? It's truth and knowledge, global power, as soft as pillows – that is what we – I – enable. And the goddam money – it comes in like leaves that's brown and withered. But the networks grow, soon everyone will be tied on – but oh no! – it's splitting up, it's all a set of fragments, cooling down already! But we must hope and plan. The unexpected isn't just disasters, it's ideas that fall into your mailbox, from anywhere at all, something to start it off again.'

He grips my arm, I feel his thigh on mine, and what comes next, I ask myself, and then he says,

'It's called a test, if you survive. It's just a thing we wizards of the infotech try out ...' and he laughs, kindly.

*

Here come some guys, they put me in a golf cart, looks as if it's bulletproof, down we go, they thrust me in a shed and clang the doors. The finest bronze. Oh no – here's giant bacteria, with their eyes and rudimentary feet – at first they stare, but now they're stamping up and down, they're only destined to be power source, that they know, maybe they're aware that is their destiny. A million of them, maybe more, are raising me above the floor. They haven't shoulders, but the thrust is there. I'm metres up – the scene is porridge on the boil, the mouths that pop and tiny eyes like husks that blink ... what can they want? It's maybe nothing much, just nasty instinct, like the horrors in the old-time movies, no plan beyond the massacre, invasion, gluten pouring in the mosques – maybe there's no intelligence, not much at least, no myth, no songs, no good fortune – forward they go, and if they're vanquished, in life there's always more, though in the movies when one lot goes down, the titles roll, The End, and out you go for drinks. But here – it seems they have a kind of plan, they're dividing, multiplying into different kinds of bugs, here comes the living mud, carnivorous flowers, the worms like sewer pipes, and maybe buggy generals and viruses first class, and flags and anthems, presidents, elections too – and what's before them isn't death and sprawl, extermination and the rest, but messages and dialogues, interviews and such.

They raise me up – we're at the roof, my! – what excitement, but they crush me to the silver, I can't turn my head, by chance my onion breath seems toxic – and so they cast me down. We're on the floor, but – oh no, the doors are locked and fast. They're safe inside, but still quite curious, intent.

A bunch of them is tugging at me, and I see – they have a key, and they unlock the door, and let me free. 'You see!' says Marlin – 'They're much brighter than the threatening kind of bug there used to be. They don't provoke. And wow! – they think,' and on he goes.

I ask, 'You think they'll save us, rescue all mankind?' He says,

'No, I don't imagine so. Why do you think they should?'

*

'Well,' says Marlin, 'For what it's worth, you passed the test, though what was tested, who can tell?'

'They have this key,' I say.

'Yes, yes,' says Marlin hastily. 'We've plans for them, those things inside, but they've no plans for us. They only need to think of after. They're the survivors. Our successors.'

There's no chair anywhere, not at his table, no prints even on its crystal top. He says,

'Candy, by the way – she doesn't think of after,' and he whispers from afar, 'She is a druggie. Stay away from her! We only do drugs for enlightenment – but she, what could she do with light, even if she finds some?'

He moves around, encircles, like a chesspiece he manoeuvres me, he's put me nearly out the door, his hand comes out as if to shake, and when I move my arm, retracts. He says,

'I get quite tired, with giving things away,' – the whispering in the panelling cuts off and servants' ears switch on. The handouts. He says,

'It is my lymph that I donate. It isn't cash, it's essence,' and the fumbling, buzzing sound resumes. There is a slot, with papers silent streaming out and flop into a bin: 'It never stops,' he says, 'it's just one flash I need, a candle flame that flares, illumines all. Genius, the inspiration – the little messages that flitter by – "how are you, what you do?" – to make them even faster, fuller still of human pith...'

I'm moved, I want to comfort him, I say, 'A new invention – that just means more cash, more stress to give it all away. I know it's what the great men do ...' and there's excursion from a shed below, explosion, some fresh brainy beast, a prototype gone critical, has bust the lock, the guys with shotguns start to move. And Marlin says,

'One day, far far away, I may be gone, and then those crawly things will rule the world for centuries. Just think of that, my friend. By then, you will be dead, but even so, you'll know – I held the line!' He draws up to his great height, a Pomeranian guardsman – his gaze on military roads ...

'You're careful about your food, I hope?' he asks me, kindly: 'It's perilous I know, but better not to give it up completely. Maybe – beans is the thing, the new, the lasting, thing,' and he takes one from a pocket, where it's been bulging, an improbable nipple: 'Look – the engineering. Each one, in itself and for itself, turned so beautifully, each one polished – not by hand, I hope, but see the speckles, and the umbilical. We could do better, I am sure, but ...' and his gaze dulls, head droops, no longer Pomeranian, just born in Hungary of parents not Hungarian – 'Better for what?'

'With pasta,' I say eagerly, 'or just a thread of oil and raw – or Bosnian bean soup, Mongolian hotpot, wow! an invention and a blessing,' and I go on, enthused.

He brings me down: 'Or peas. Pack some for your route – the customs shouldn't care. They fill the corners of your case. And in a year or so, we'll meet again, and you can put the mail in there,' and he points to the bin: 'I don't expect the new idea will germinate in Ulan Bator, but you never know.'

*

Candy says, 'He quite likes you,' and I say,

'Great men, they quite like everyone, until they don't,' – she says that is the price, my risk, I'm quite an ordinary guy, it's nice to find one for a change, if not for long, and then I tell her – my exploits, friends gone lost, and women too, the fates escaped, the gods propitiated, Death put on hold, disasters various – and she's impressed, and pulls away, and says, 'Be careful what you do, Marlin's not the type who easily forgives,' and I say, 'That's me too – I can't forget the future or the past,' and then the brother calls again, maybe she has a caring side? – and then she switches off her phone.

Marlin thinks I'm out to steal his girl, his cash – his core. He thinks I'll cheat him, not picking up his mail, and make a fool of him. Candy says,

'You can't steal me.'

I say, 'Not exactly theft I have in mind for you. What interests me's – the new boss class. The guys like Marlin think there's a new power, ideas, that they've invented. His genius. But in the end it's all just cash and hiring guys, and brushing poor ones off his limousine ...' and she says,

'In the end, you need an army – maybe you don't call it that, but guys in uniform with guns, and all the rest. So – where's the harm, and where's the new?'

What I have in mind to steal is not his time, his judgement – but his mail. Of course, I'll do my round.

'He has a vision, Marlin does,' she says: 'The message of messages won't come the modern way, but on a postcard. Something special and remote – like those babies in the East who know four thousand lines of verse at birth, and tame the elephants by whispering up their trunks.' She peers at me:

'That adventure in the shed – maybe you got a little colonised? Our successors there – they raised you up, against the silver roof?'

'Yes – I don't know how to react to that.'

'They eat the stuff that grows on silver – it was a dinner invite,' Candy says.

'That was nice of them, exceptional,' I say, 'Although...'

'You shouldn't take it as a friendly act, still less they'd want to know you. They may have got inside you – it happens to me when I eat with guys. Boy – I should know!' and she waggles herself, quite irresistible, though I resist. She says,

'You've heard of Klein bottles, I dare say, the rubber things, that's only got one side. They're quite like us, we humans. If those guys have got inside, we'll have to bath you,' and she looks inspired: 'It's not a thing that I can do myself, I fear,' and here come guys, they set things up, an urnlike article, for tea, for burials too, maybe.

They cram me in, and turn it on, it isn't hot or cold, it's like a finger going down your throat and reaching down and down, your ankles, they're a crucial point – a twist, it's at your toes ... I hear her, talking on and on, of how those postal drops, they change, and she may come and check if Marlin won't – Lanzhou and Cobalt, Tomich, Baku – there's genius in every fold of landscape, wanting to make its mark, a postcard in the blue.

Then the finger starts to draw and pull – I'm turning inside out, the organs that you hope to hide, they all pop out, the colours marvellous, the purple, orange, fox-brown, the red of copper shawms, and things like runner-beans that throb – green outside, amber in – and all a-shake and pulsing, all wired up, cooperative, like a production line, a bit precarious, – for Studebakers perhaps, buttocks upholstered as their seats.

'Whatever can I look like, Candy,' I exclaim. It doesn't hurt, but what I am is not in dreams, I'm like a building with its pipes and conduits hung outside – and now some guys are combing me, and what's inside is now turned inside out, the gut, the heart, and now the brain – oh, how embarrassing, and every thought is fingered through, and every rivulet of memory is sluiced and flooded, who can tell where it flows out, maybe this urn contains a tap – and every error, every slip, faux pas, the acts of faith misplaced or lied about, they're all scoured out, and trickle down, away.

It turns me right way back. The hand – can't be the hand of God, I think – it brings me right, blotched, scarred and greyish-green again, here comes the skin, there go the lungs all honeycombed like tripes, back go the guts, the ganglia all fire, the knees click back, the fluids make a joyous sound, and here I am again, the other me, the outer. Outside, I hear–

'Is he my clean boy now?' It's Marlin. Candy says,

'He didn't graze on patina, on hornsilver, so he is quite pure, reamed out. We've decolonised him out and in, his analytic skills are polished up,' and on she goes...

'You shouldn't feel embarrassed,' Candy says. 'Your appendix now – a lovely seahorse shape, pink like a coral bead, a question mark amidst the rest of you – that stuff like bellows, stoves industrial, the sparking plugs – it stands out modest, true. I've seen a side of you that others miss,' and she hugs me to her, and hums a little – 'I've looked at life from both sides now ...' and I say,

'I guess you've all been through it,' and she says,

'Of course not, silly, we should all be dead ... It's you that has the quest ahead, so – better face it clean.'

*

'You understand,' says Candy. 'Whatever projects you might have – are made redundant by our own. Creating survivors, the new forms when yours have croaked ...' and Marlin says,

'That's why we have to clean you out. In the sheds, those guys just eat and eat.'

I ask, 'Then in the end, there'll just be one big hungry one that's left. It's useful for the movie, but ...'

'No, no,' he says. 'They reproduce as well – more and more, bigger and bigger,' and I say,

'Why don't you eat one, have it live inside, and then – you've got the future bottled up. Life everlasting, or at least quite long. Why bother with the postcards?'

'Come, come,' says Candy. 'Think of the philosophy! You can't have someone in two provinces of time at once!' She whispers, 'Besides, it's all hypothesis – you can't believe that eating silver brightens up those bugs? Next time you're in there – watch out, they're not our friends, don't even use the word.'

Marlin listens in, he says, 'Don't underestimate the power of silver – I may send you round the mines to check. There's Hungary, Potosi, the Panshir – the chemistry, the compounds ...'

'But I don't believe,' I say, and he goes on,

'Then there's the larger beasts, the other sheds. Some go forward, others back. No problem of philosophy,' and he scowls at Candy. A little wearily, it seems. She says,

'I need to know your background, if you're going round the silver mines.' I tell her,

'Russia, Mexico – a guy reminding us of Trotsky, though not like him at all. Myself – not like anyone.'

'Right, right,' she says. 'That's background done, and quite enough. I'll find out more, that's how it goes with travelling. Some of the path is mine as well,' and so we're friends, it seems.

*

'There is no hope,' cries Marlin, rushing up: 'We're going out of orbit! Maybe that is best, and quick,' and Candy turns to him and then to me, and gives us hugs. He rushes out, and Candy says, 'It often happens so – he slides a dot, his fingers stick on buttons – and we're off,' and sure, he's back

'A false alarm,' he says. 'But how I hate this adding up. This science for tomorrow – what it means for me is torturing the beasts. We took the birds, and now there's hope by eating junk they will be dinosaurs again, but shall we see it? Shall we?' and he thrusts his face in mine. 'What's that?' he asks, and answers, 'A reek. Of onions. Very wise. An ancient thing; the pyramids were built by guys who hefted blocks of two tons each – all done by onions,' and he talks of breakfasts, then,

'I'm not a happy man,' he says.

I say, 'Drugs, revolutions – that's the world I know. All this is weird – you mobilise your brain to make us guys survive, but then you bet the other side, the things that will succeed us when we're gone. It makes no sense. The mail – you don't need me to run around the world – just get some counter guy to send it on ...' and Marlin interrupts,

'Haha! I see you're not an artist – it is the chrism of the unforeseen, the postcard coming from the sticks, my fellow genius who doesn't trust the messaging. And I should know – that's my invention, quick thoughts and carefree, that electric stuff, goddam it, all those cracks, the losses through the floorboards, stuff getting lost, the best of it ... The genius that saves the world! The new idea! It's on a postcard revelation will descend ...' and on he goes.

*

It seems old Franco's up in court, those stolen books ... and Candy says,

'You're keen on justice, help him out. It's written on you, so you say. It's in your skin. A story for the judge – that is the least that you, the just one, owes.'

I say, 'I tried to cheat him out his room,' and Candy says,

'That doesn't mean a thing, what's cheating got to do with justice? Get the poor guy off the charge, and that's enough.'

We go to court – the city we pass through is full of life just as it was, those centuries before. There is the opera church, the streets that once were practice tracks for chariots, here the barracks for the drivers and the gladiators – here the room where Franco reads ...

They fit me on a tight gold tunic in the court. I say,

'Old Franco's books can't be unglued, and so we can't identify the crime,' and there's a laugh, and we'll go back in ten or twenty years when we've unstuck the evidence. Old Franco says, 'I've found out why Rome fell – they hadn't thought of landfill, so the houses rose on rubbish, rubbish metres thick, miasma – sometimes boosted you, but mostly left you feverish, lethargic – so it all came down, or rather, all went up, until the Colosseum, built to hold the refuse, was the only building standing and above ground, even that was blown apart by gas, and so it ended. Empire. Landfill. That's the thing would save them, but in the end ...' And he goes happy home.

*

Marlin says, 'I think I'm gay, at heart – but Candy here, who can resist her retro stuff? – besides, I've other guesses I must make, hypotheses, all that. First – we don't want our soldiers here. Degenerates. Why don't they go and camp in other people's lands?'

I ask, 'Why do you think of that, the soldiery? Look – Candy's clothes light up our eyes – no military there,' – and she is into Sixties stuff, a green angora sweater, on her breasts laid out in silver twine '*bonne chance*'. She shows them off, and says, 'I'd love love stories with a someone,' and I think,

'Oh no, if she binds in with Marlin tight, all my schemes are compromised – and if it's me she hooks on, well, what a bore, and parting in some diner, maybe that waiter guy will jostle you and make you fall, down the front steps, cadaver, off in the forest to be buried – there's no witches now, with huts, but they will spade you in among the trees, and in a while you'll be foundations of a kiosk ...' I say, 'No, no, too much romance, dear Candy, it embitters you. And why this talk of soldiers now?'

She says, 'There's a balance to be struck – a somewhere place, to find between the soldiers and the enemies. A compromise – armed guys. My scene. Marlin just gets to do the sums, he's into *pax eterna*. That's some hope! Other science guys, they come, they argue, check the figures,' and she waves her hands, it's vague, but still an indication.

'Candy,' I say, later, relaxed, 'not to be personal – but what a funny body you have there.'

She laughs.

'Don't you like it? You'll acquire the taste – it's retro, all last century, exciting, if you weren't around ... Modifications can be made, but only if I'm suited.'

*

Later still, and more relaxed, we talk of futures, and she says,

'We were looking for an idiot. Then you came along.'

I say, 'Sometimes I've had the feeling you were making fun of me.'

'Well, not just you, but all your baggage train – it's like old Franco, stolen books and shorter civilisations: the justice and the quest. All right in their place, it's just the place is never found.'

'We'll do the science and the future, you do security,' she says.

'The postcards? The thumbprints?' I ask.

'The new ideas? Yes, always on the lookout. But – everyone has a network, everyone who can. You – must assemble squads, around the world, and let us have their prints. Loyal guys, ready for the worst, and that will surely come! Guys we will possess,' she says.

I say, 'Your stuff's here, in those sheds – who'd want to take that off, who'd dare attack, and let it out? And if they try – they'd need to be a state, an army.'

'There's always someone, wants to take you over, that's what Marlin says. Or you need a place to run. With guys you trust,' says Candy.

I say, 'Suppose then, you're attacked, there's danger – guys ill-intentioned ...'

'We shoot them. Our guys, that is – they shoot the enemy. It's always so,' she says. 'It's history.'

I say, 'Maybe I should have kept – companions. Someone to travel with. All those old friends ...' She laughs, 'Remember – three strikes, you're out. And you've had more than three. Your destiny. But – I can always visit,' and I say,

'Yes, the novelty, new guys, the genius – but you're retro, Candy. You don't fit,' and she laughs again, and says,

'Me? Retro? It's a fashion statement, stuff from way back, when I wasn't born. Before the freedom. I still know what's new.'

'But ...' I say.

'Just do it,' says Candy. 'No going back. Recruit determined guys. No pay, just orders. Loyalty. Lots of loyalty, then maybe pay. No fine ideas.'

'You're warlords, for when it all starts coming down?' I say.

'We've bet against the species, that is true. But first, to defend our interests ...'

'Those look good to me right now,' I say.

Marlin concludes: 'It's like she says. Do it. No introspection, I've been all through that, it doesn't change a thing.'

*

I fly off, starting with a country 'A'. Then, up this stony track – ah, here's a guy, expectant, persecuted maybe. Looks like a Zoroastrian. I tell him all.

'There's always battles,' he says. 'Why should I sign up for more?' I say,

'You Zoroaster guys, you rest on battles – there's the battle of religion, and the final one – last times. The threats, the people with the parted hair, the wolves with two legs, and with four. The people in the red carts too,' but –

'No, no,' he interrupts. 'The carts – that wasn't us. But now – no battles, each will lie up in their tower: the end, the birds to pick you clean ...' and I think of Gabrielle, her 'fuck the birds'.

Zoroastrians – fled north to where the pomegranates grow. This guy – gives me a bright red fruit: those are the best, round-cut rubies crammed within.

He says, 'Why don't your masters use the telephone to order soldiers, like the others do? The world is full of them,' and it's true. The rest is messages without a messenger.

He says they must want something more – a secret band, an oath

'Who'd want to do battle for Marlin Corp?' he asks, and that's true too – no politics, religion not required, the corp has not a border, not a bomb to drop or stop, they defend no rich and terrorise no poor. There must be something more they want ...

'Maybe they don't know what they want,' he says.

That is true. It will be written on a postcard. That's for sure.

'This place – was paradise then,' he says. 'In bible times. But it hasn't been so for a while,' and we look over a dead land, where a line of trench remains, bulging where the braver had dug faster.

'I'm sure those two both knew what pomegranates lead to,' he says, pointing to two ancient people not in sight. 'You couldn't watch those apples growing here, without becoming curious. And hungry too. Good and evil – in the fruit? or in the tree? Or Spirit, sprayed on, like insecticide? It's a way of putting blame on women – and on snakes.'

I think of Candy – not a scientist – maybe expert in the evil and the good. The sheds … where snakes are raised, and things like snakes, that wrap around you, need the heat of humankind.

The guy says, 'I think we've gone as far as reason takes. They say we set ourselves only the problems we can solve. That's a reassurance, but it can't be true for ever – some problems we don't see until they're on us, and we shunt the harder ones still further back,' and to cut him short I say,

'But we can eat the fruit. You need to chase those birds away.'

'Here,' he says. 'Take this fruit, the reddest one – you say it gives you good and evil both? That means – it doesn't solve a thing, this knowledge is a con – they say it's clear, but no! you have to sort out the which is which, the good, the bad. The answer's not just in the fruit – besides, I promise you, my pomegranates, they're all good!'

I write down 'doubtful' for our cause, this Zoroastrian. Candy joins me, and we talk of Eden, those two guys. She says,

'Of course, those were just prototypes – it went bad almost from the start. Their line, that Eve and him – I guess it's still around – they bet on work and being good. Lenin, he had them in mind. But then ... quite soon, all other types of guy emerged. Think of Vienna: what an enterprise! 1900! The critical glance, the story underneath the petticoats, the goatees, those cigars. Unhappy products – that's the flaw. Those kinds of humans – how'd they cope with bible ones?'

'Candy,' I say. 'It's all in stereotypes.' She laughs.

'It's reason, stupid – if you don't think with that, the reasoning, you don't get anywhere. Myself yes, I'd have followed Zoroaster – fire, that is the thing. Purity is what you need,' but that's not my scenario, and I say,

'It seems so hard that lots of guys are settling down, and have some stuff to eat at last, and buy in stores, and now it's coming to an end,' and she says,

'Cut that capitalistic crap – it's not like you. And no, the problem is that all the products, models – humans, as we call them, they're all let out and live with difficulty together – simultaneously, side by side, and flying round, in trains and such. The problem is the difference, how it grates. Simplicity is what you need, what Marlin's info gives – a little message, you exchange your news, it can't be much. Two simpletons – no snake. But then – out on the street you go, and there's fire guys, and the guys that shakes, and some with many heads and arms, and some with faces upward turned – some gods, some demons. And the void ...'

I say, 'But that is all religions, Candy, we know all that – it's history,' but she shouts and says,

'No, no, it's differences, you fool, it's character. It's guys with swords and guys with clubs, and guys with coins and guys with jugs of wine. You need to simplify – the only way to look for truth. You need protection, too. I see you try so hard to come to terms with modern things. New stuff, and what will come after it. You're pitiful, but also ... no, sweet's not the word. Rather – ingratiating. As if it's all there to save you, and to sweep you all away.'

I say, irritated, 'Well, for the moment, we're human. When your monsters stretch their wings ...' and I don't know how to finish. I think of love-apples, pomegranates, all the stories we've attached to them. I say, 'I may not be up to everything that happens,' but that does sound pathetic, and I think of times when things were harsh, and I was harsher with them; of Russia, and of Mexico.

'Fuck you, Candy,' I say. 'You hedge your bets, but in the race those horses – there are always more, not all can be discounted.' I think of what waits in the sheds, and Marlin thrown down on his back and struggling with the raging feisty stuff that riots out.

*

Candy and I – we fly some more.

## Egypt

'Your room smells of camels,' I say, though my thoughts are with my onions.

'It's that guy,' she says. 'He takes people to the pyramid.'

'You should watch how you pick up lovers,' I say, 'Or you might get entanglements.'

'I hate romantics, and their whiff,' says Candy, 'Though some animals don't smell. Trotsky's rabbits, for one,' and she laughs at me.

'It's true, Mexico's a hard place,' I say. 'But even rabbits smell, if you love them, and are close to them.'

'As a recruiter,' Candy says, 'you're a dog that never leaves the trap! We want loyal guys, not weird ones from the marches. Soldiers – that's the type. They're beetles – see how they dress, those hats, the armour and the wingcases ... They eat the dead, that's what they're for, and sweep a space for innovation.'

I say, 'It's still a mystery, why you should want them – soldiers, they are not your type. You like the things that's overripe, guys that attract a buzz of parasites ...'

'That's you all right,' she says, 'a parasite.' I'm irritated, and I say,

'I'm quite the soldier type: destroy, create. An artist, too. '"I walk, mainly I walk" – that is the sterling point. That's why we – they – need our boots. Remember what they say – "The soldier – lives and shoots to make money: – but he should not under any circumstances make money in order to live and shoot." That's how it goes. Maybe that's why your scheme and mine don't fit.'

'My dear,' she says, 'I need a hand, not argument. I didn't eat that guy, the camel guy. But you can guess, these local guys – you need to dispose of them, but they're so tough, they argue, they resist.'

'Show me,' I say. I'm quite resigned to cleaning up, leaving this place, full so it seems of people, nothing much to do, and we should travel West, I think to Senegal, pulled on by the music, seeking loyalty. A place to start from.

'He's in this wardrobe,' Candy says, and so he is. She's stabbed him through and through – a soldier's trick.

We don't clean up, we leave him, and she pays the bill, and I explain that's how life goes, you try explaining life to some guys, it's hopeless, and I say,

'You owe me, Candy,' and she says,

'Recruiting guys – that is your task. It seems you don't believe. Not in that, not much. Explaining life to you's impossible, it's hopeless.'

So, on we go. We're the soldier and the tourist both: we – they – leave the bodies where they slump, and no one counts and no one cares, and Candy says,

'It's like that Zoroaster said – that battle in the last times – you must give no quarter,' and I think of lying there, up on the platform in the tower, eyes wide, unclosing, waiting for the birds to come and start.

'Hmmm,' says Candy. 'Trotsky found a path. It didn't lead far.'

'You shouldn't have killed that guy,' I say. 'It'll follow us around.'

'I couldn't get rid of him. He spoke of love and life thereafter. So – I got rid of him. You're maybe jealous, silly boy? Here, there's too many cops – you know, the crimes are solved when there's just one. In all the books, it's so. One cop. When there's a crew, they make a mess.'

I say, 'He surely had a family, or some guys to stand for him,' and then I see – that's how a network grows. And loyalty, and missions too. It must start with a death, unseen or senseless – that's the core, and all rolls up around it. So – 'Candy, you're a genius. Death's the starting point,' I say, but she objects – it's Marlin sees the panorama, she just deals with gangs and bands, commissioning the guys that make the sheds and find her retro stuff.

*

Marlin flies to see us. We shout across a perspex screen. 'I can't land properly,' he says. 'I'd have to bring five millions – for investment. I'm departing now – but Candy! – how impulsive! Death. A driver, though, he didn't own his camel. Camels, tourists – oh my dear!'

'Don't bring class in,' Candy says. 'And we need protection ...'

'Well,' Marlin says, 'on the plane I read this book, some guy, El something, a great detective, bit morose. And all those people, all those names ... but in the end,' and Candy shouts,

'And in the end!? A book, a story.'

Marlin says, 'You're sure it's not hallucination, all of it?' and she says,

'Well, that's definitions again. But now – we're off to Senegal,' and I add,

'And Chad. It's for the music—'

'You're deviating now, you clowns,' Marlin interrupts. 'The idea was – a chain of criminals and feisty guys with guns, like all the other big guys, corporations, have, and not to mention states and such, for when the last times come – the crowds, the rationing, the goddam heat or cold. Not to mention – what we do, experiments. Science. The things that will replace the species, us. But now ... this dead guy ...'

'Now, it fits,' says Candy proudly: 'We've got the crime, is what they call it – really exasperation, maybe we should have found a space ... those camels know the pyramids, just dump the corpse in one, it's what they're for, there must be room.'

'Well,' says Marlin, 'you should know all kinds of guy by now to help you out. Me, I just know the brainy ones, and they're no use with murdered bodies ...'

Candy interrupts, 'Who else, if not them?'

I say, 'I met a guy, when I was in Armenia,' and I tell Marlin about the fire, the bright red pomegranate, the birds, the lying on your back, eyes open to the sky, the light, the beaks. Vultures, if you can. He doesn't seem to listen, and he says,

'I'm flying back. A plane, so fuck the birds. Just sort it out. My disappointment, Candy, take it with you, all around the globe.'

*

'Next,' says Candy, as we flee through Chad, 'There's a temple where there's rats and swans. And souls on lotuses. How come, around the world there's guys inventing all this stuff?'

I say, 'There's who bets on *dharma*, and the Buddha who returns to earth. That guy up there – Armenia – the fire-and-light guy – had it right. It's all outcomes, Candy. People keep their hope and twist it into shapes, and sing and shout, – it's all about the endgame,' but she's not satisfied:

'I haven't heard of half these saviours – who are they, where'd we find them?' and I say,

'Your problem is Khalid. Guy in the wardrobe,' and she cries,

'Oh – help me, help me, save and protect me! You could be, yes, yes, you are! my minister of war. A minister of state. That guy Khalid was fine and fun, but he had sticky ways. I said I'd like a monument – not exactly pyramids for me and Marlin, but let's say a hologram. And he laughed, and said that camels would devour it, all our memories and what we'd done, we're just a tasty mirage in the sand. And yes, he was a lovely guy, but he deserved ...' and on she goes. I say,

'What you offer me is dross. All your efforts point away, towards a future we don't see.' She weeps and says,

'You can't be sure,' but I am angry, there in Chad we didn't find a soul I knew. Postcards are not enough, and down I've gone, into their traps – Candy and Marlin, they have sticky ways, you're caught up in their round – their goddam gadgets and the messages. The people wheel and fan like clouds of starlings – no one's the leader, but they're led. All follow, shifting shapes, the vortices ...

The cash – it still comes in. We fly, we land, we flee, and Candy says,

'It's all good fun, though if we're caught, I fear the worst. What will you do? For I've the cash, and you? Still nothing?' and it's true, and unequivocal. A truth old-fashioned, inescapable.

'Khalid? He just laughed?' I ask, 'It seems a little thing. A comic cosmic thing. That'll teach him, if somewhere he exists to learn.'

Candy says, 'You are our general – you must be used to burials. And blame.'

'There was no burial. There is no blame,' I say.

'Well, surely some, a little. For us, the team,' she says.

'No,' I say. 'No blame.'

'You'll have to wait and see,' she says.

'It is a triumph of the indeterminate,' I say. Lightening up. Candy's my goldmine, in her tortuous galleries I kneel, follow the ore, scrabbling and sweating. I'm owned, possessed: without a contract.

'He could be mummified by now,' she says. 'They all know how to do it there, and in a thousand years – that wardrobe – it'll bring the tourists in, and I'll be free ...'

She adds, 'It's like they say, the messenger's the message, we stand proud and firm, angels of death, that's what we are,' and we fly on, we sleep and wash our clothes in aeroplanes, our bodies soften into lazy shapes, we flee from no one – no detective, with gun or guess, is following. I say,

'Candy, you're overheating,' and she says,

'No, no, a plane is taking wing, it waits for us – Nagpur,' and so I tell her,

'Candy, those cards you use to pay – if guys are interested, they can see where we have been. It's Marlin's best invention ... flying plastic carpets,' and she says,

'That idiot! His gadgets – they will bring our death in double time and – oh no! Khalid! Suppose I'm pregnant with his camel?' and we laugh, it is the cure, they say, and though it is a lie I reassure,

'The guys that mix with tourists – they are prudent, Candy,' then,

'Candy, it's so retro, back to humans, networks of loyal guys. It's clans and tribes,' and she is irritated, and she says,

'Well, what did you expect? Now, off to Mumbai – there's fine slums where we can hide and maybe eat, recruit some wise men, maybe place some bets on monkeys – they may try again, another route, an evolution, end up better than we are ...' and on she goes.

At last, I say, 'If only you weren't so tall, we shouldn't suffer so. The flying. Meant for immaterials.'

'That's true,' she says. 'In height, I'm made for Marlin. Makes me feel remote,' but now she looks down from the windows, less scared of seeing sleuths. 'Down there, down there,' she cries, and we see soldiers scuttling round in windowless machines – you'd think you need to see outside, the dangers! These goddam planes instead – there's panorama all around, and not a thing to see. She says,

'Field marshals, generals – yes, the ones that win are *generally* short,' and laughs – a play on words uncoupled – 'Land here,' she says, and so we do.

'I want to lend a hand,' she says. 'These guys are fighting hard, but from up high we see far better than they do – where they're off to, and all that.'

She's tall as a queen, tall as a stork. A face that's made by jewellers. Baby camels, pouched and hidden somewhere intimate.

Now, here's a line of cops, they seek assassins, but she tells them, 'We're here to look for wise men,' and they defer to her and snap us with their telephones.

Ah! Revolution!

'This lot, this lot,' she shouts. 'Marlin should be here, and give this lot some cash. Their cause is doubtless just.'

Who can resist the call – to justice? Candy can't. I'd rather go on, see the temple, monkeys busy with the catering, the pilgrims coming up those thousand steps with nothing, going home with little cakes inside, the nothing satisfied and smiling now.

'This is the real, I'd recognise it anywhere,' she says. 'There's lots of killing going on, and no one takes your name or counts the rounds you shoot, they have machines that fork the dead in those pits there, and everyone keeps quiet about the things they see and do. And so, I'll maybe join them, be the queen,' and on she goes. I say,

'You should forget that guy, Khalid – for sure, he wasn't just. Don't enthuse, don't over-compensate. He's just a casual casualty,' and so she laughs, and says I'm in the spirit of her language jokes, and laughter smooths things out – and yes! she sees her army now, she is the queen from heaven, bringing cash.

'Charge!' shouts Candy, running halfway up the slope: 'This is the modern way, not sneaking round the back. Remember,' she calls to few guys slinking after, 'The landscape is your friend, your mother. It lives! It's full of mind – use it, it takes care of you.'

'There!' she says, returning to me, 'This is real life! These guys – they risk their lives, they're sure they're on the right, the just, path,' and I say,

'I've done all this before. Who knows how it turns out?'

'Of course you have,' she says. 'It turns out well for you – you're here, and accidents, they haven't happened yet. It's useless to predict,' and on she talks, freewheeling, how an evening's fun can cast you down, but lifetime in an army's quite determinate and dull – and so I see Khalid go sliding into accident and 'who'd have thought ...' It's good she's free of him, I guess. These guys are waving freedom flags. Each to be free, or all? – and then she says, 'Each one is made exact, the mirror of the guy that's next, before and after, and so worthy of the same respect, and that is being free and justice too,' and she's the queen, and there's no argument.

'That stick,' I say. 'You charged with it.'

'So I see,' says Candy. 'A fine stick, worthy of the fine words we went with.'

'I'm not sure you're worthy of the words,' I say. 'And – no "we". I didn't charge.'

We stare at the stick. It's been lying around – teak, or olive, you see where twigs or leaves began, or might begin. A thing that gives authority. Amusement even – or just whittling away some time. A baton – orchestras, field marshals – or wand and magic.

'I am there,' says Candy – 'How amazing! A vision! I am there, in your garden, place d'armes, there, holding the stick, in your memory-space. And – what if you forget, expunge me? Where should I be?'

I've no response to this. I say, 'Maybe those fine things, the freedom, justice – maybe after all they're not worth you shouting out.'

'That's rather arrogant,' she says.

'That's not what I meant,' I say. 'They're not some things that you can see. They're things you shout.' Then,

'The charge. Why only halfway up?' I ask. 'That rules out a sequence, picture, purpose. It leaves you stuck between the stick and triumph.'

'It's a fine stick,' she says, waving it: 'It's not a weapon, it's protection, a talisman. Could be my immunity.'

'It's the same as with your murder,' I say, 'Required, at the time, not necessary.'

'I don't see that,' she says. 'Don't go on. You could have asked the detail while it happened. What you say, what you ask, now it doesn't change a thing.'

'I'm not so sure,' I say. 'It changes everything – everything that can be changed.'

'No,' she says. 'I won't follow there. We need height and speed, the distance. Back to the planes.'

'We're not doing Marlin's work,' I say.

'No. Maybe he doesn't mind.'

'Where next?' I ask. 'You can't say you're fleeing justice ...'

'No, no,' she says. 'It's flying! The speed, the going – no place to no place, all different, all the same. The bending over, peering down at creeping stuff. And – how could I flee from justice, when you are the just?'

'It depends,' I say. 'On what your story is. And the punishment?'

'No, no,' she says, 'It's justice that I want, not punishment.'

'What is your story, then?' I ask.

'It's not decided yet,' she says. 'For sure, that guy Khalid – he was determined and determinate – the truth was written over him, though not upon his skin.'

'You're just like Marlin, then,' I say, 'It's indeterminacy you want, that way you're never caught.'

'No, no,' she says. 'Not Marlin! Everything is open-ended for him, he can't conclude. Even in our bed ...' I interrupt,

'This new idea that we are seeking, then – the search is inconclusive?' and she shouts,

'You idiot! The new thing could be tiny! He won't specify – negligible or immense, it's all the same,' and I say,

'Candy, don't shout. Emotion on the plane – you mustn't show. They'll throw us off,' and so they do. We glide right down – it's a relief, and doesn't cost. It seems we're in a compound – could be temples, could be military – goat haven, there are plenty here, and Candy says,

'These soldiers – and the revolution that I tried my hand at – they can't do a thing, those guys, what moves today is cash that flows around like blood, and guys that have their demos in the street and have no fear – you shoot them down, and they are bakers and mechanics, so you can't eat or drive around in limousines,' and she is right, and that is how things are. You take the military road, it's like the Path, it ends for ever, like the sea, and starts for ever ...

'You must see the Major: MacTaggart,' says a guy with stripes.

*

The Major wears a tag. He doesn't look like a MacTaggart.

'In the last resort,' he says, 'we decide what goes down and what stays up, and who. Then, orders come. There is singing too – folk come from everywhere – to see the goats, to seek a sanctuary. To feel secure.'

I ask, 'And do they come from Chad?'

'Oh no,' he says, 'It's mostly classical. Retro is in, they want the young to use their diaphragms. Electric twangling – it's quite out.'

The soldiers here – they're well hooked up and messaged in.

'I see Marlin on this little screen,' says Candy, 'There he is, a-potter round his sheds. And shakes his fists. Frustration. My, how the silver glints and gleams, the bronze resounds, I'll bet the patina is scoffed at once, those bugs – what housekeepers,' and she weeps, she laughs, the world is smaller that a nut, it seems, its kernel full of hungry life.

'It's here, here, I feel it,' Candy says. 'Here is a repository, here culture passes through, though not from Chad, it seems, which I regret ... And values. Shooting at the bad and the obsessed. Who could object? It's quite precise – you shoot, the prize is peace, at least a deal. You see MacTaggart's finger, pressing on the scales.'

'The trigger too,' I say, but Candy hushes me, she says, 'These guys – they are true pacifists, peace their goal – not like you, you opportunist!' I'm indifferent, she employs me, after all, and other idiots too. 'And yet,' I say, 'the mechanism is not clear. The story is not wholly told – it's like your murder, Candy,' and MacTaggart says,

'If you're concerned, we have a court here that will sort things out, and after, celebration or cells, you take your chance,' and Candy says,

'Oh no, this guy here, in my employ – he is the just. He would hand some justice out – except he's waiting, waiting for the story to be told,' and MacTaggart laughs, he is a little guy and laughter shakes him up – he says he'll show us where his justice works, but Candy says that's just banal and cloudy – we are here to see the new that leaches into future lives and places far away in time that we can't go, but mere material bangs and thrash, those don't concern us.

MacTaggart seems offended, and he says, 'There's the Idea! It's real as bangs! It's matter too, and quite demanding. You must be ubiquitous – before the bangs, behind them too. Not security alone, but justice too.'

He lines up a bunch of guys, and off we go.

'I see no goats,' I say, the file goes stumbling down a stony path, with crosses either side, to mark where guys have fallen – shot or tumbled down.

'The people here,' MacTaggart pants, 'not only tell tall tales, they steal. The goats – we store them all inside, impounded, promoting social peace ... Not true we've stolen them,' and we are satisfied, and Candy strides along, a standard, looking straight ahead. I'm humming, '*non m'affligge il tormento di morte*' – 'Not the torment of death afflicts me, but my beloved, her tormenting' ... My singer, Candy's brother: where can they be? Then –

'Oh no!' we cry: a shelf of grey-black scree's detached – it's like South Georgia, those penguins hanging on the slopes, its tiny post office, bravely flagged, maybe a guy inside to take the new idea, the postcard – us hoping that he doesn't steal the notion, keep it as his own. Oh no! we skitter down, Candy, the warriors, me, MacTaggart, his boots, buffed and huffed upon by some poor guy, a private, mortgaged in his privacy, his duty just to polish up MacTaggart. How those eyelets shine! And oh, the dust, the pointed stones...

'Well,' says MacTaggart, 'any of you guys in doubt – materialism allows no compromise of time and place?' and all survivors shout, 'Yes, yes,' as they've been trained to do, and we are landed in the village street, defenders of ideas, a crossroads for the music here, classical, progressive too.

MacTaggart says, 'Candy – you'll want to send a message through to Marlin, you being his beloved – a reassure?'

'Fuck Marlin,' Candy says. 'Some guys tried to blow us up.'

MacTaggart laughs, and says, 'It's gravity, my dear, it happens all the time – the infrastructure here is crap,' – do we believe him? – and villagers crowd round, with little telephones they snap and send. MacTaggart says,

'With terror, as with torment, you don't joke,' and that is true. 'You're fortunate,' he says. 'You're free and irresponsible – I have to make a count and reason why there's fewer coming back than started out,' and now we sit, we three, beneath a palm, and there is magic fruit and booze, for Candy's credit card is good, it is the hour to think of Rimbaud, and we do, we chant, we improvise, and this is freedom's time.

We have survived, the warriors dance, and all is as it was when first we heard of poetry and symphonies, and all the things MacTaggart loves. Candy says, 'Why don't we buy some goats, and live on here – MacTaggart to protect us, and it's quite a paradise – look, look, the snow above, blue lakes beneath, and in between – some grass.'

'There's something more,' I say to her, and she replies,

'Yes, yes, there always is. And something less. The Path – and look, it tumbled down, it is a chancy metaphor, and sometimes there is penguins, sometimes goats, but always there is goddam metaphysics – down we go! – and what's your answer, your analysis?'

She's so determined, I can't find the words. MacTaggart says, 'Just eat this fruit and drink this booze, give thanks for being saved – by me, and gravity.'

Candy peers at her little screen – it's in her palm. It's Marlin, and he shouts,

'You clowns! You stupid Jack and Jill – fell down the hill! Those guys are not our own. You've teamed up with the wrong, the rabid guys! Now, I can't go round the world, from conference to mail drop, you idiots have compromised me, joined the enemy,' and on he goes.

'The Major here – he can't be wrong,' I say. 'He's called MacTaggart,' and the screen says 'Fools!' All is quiet again, though Candy weeps.

I ask her, 'MacTaggart. Terror? Revolution? Or the contrary of both? It seems he has fixed tastes in music – that could be bigotry.'

'I thought we might recruit him,' Candy says, but I say,

'No, no, more likely he recruits us. But even in the music, our categories don't fit – yours, mine and his.'

She says, 'And so, forget all that, the goats, the falling off the trail. Just bear in mind, we breed our livestock in those sheds back home, and they are not our friends. Don't tangle into them. MacTaggart may be rabid – but if we pay him, he'll protect us as we rise or fall.'

MacTaggart doesn't listen, and he says, 'My scheme is this. First, I must choose and serve some friends. Then, select my enemies. And wild objectives. It's probable my friends become my enemies,' and he shouts: 'Revenge!'

I say, 'This here's a dump, and lots of dust. The thorn trees. That is why you're sour. There's nothing doing here, no future, just a messy here and now,' and Candy says,

'Yeah! You need some trendy stores. Guys love to buy – I haven't bought for months – just tickets, for displacements.'

'It's not that easy,' says MacTaggart, 'since we don't have stores, you need a faith, and people in their place, or else!' and Candy says,

'In that respect – we're maybe sliding back, Marlin too. The guys here, they don't care if they survive – still less they care about the species, what comes next. Is this, then, the new?' and we stare at each other, quite disconsolate. Then Candy lightens it, she says,

'Your boots, MacTaggart – revelations. They shine like eyes. How is it done? Hot spoons?'

He says, 'No, it's done by servants.'

*

'I've spoken to Marlin,' Candy says. '"Change your fashion message, if you must," he says. "No backslides though." I tell him, "Backslides – inevitable, in the scree." He laughs.'

Then, she says to me, 'MacTaggart doesn't have a room to sleep in,' and I say, 'Don't let him into yours. He has the mountain cave. It must go right through,' and so do we.

'I'm losing my direction,' Candy says. 'It's this going round with someone normal just like you – not a clue, and not a hope: just a frozen block, like they toss off planes.'

Where MacTaggart spends his time – it's once-new stuff, not unpacked, now long passed by. Blanco paste in cans, for webbing. Armourers' tools. Some swords. Bundles of Macbeth –

'Where MacTaggart finds his name,' says Candy, 'And all his military stuff.'

A single Métal Hurlant. 'Worth a fortune,' Candy says. And on and on, a box of white tiles, cool rocky alcoves – mosquitoes wrapped in dusty shrouds.

'All this, it makes me cry,' says Candy. 'This residue, unborn.'

*

'Look, MacTaggart,' I say. 'I'm not telling you this because we share the same skin colour,' and I think – Khalid's too, but that's no longer relevant: 'It's because you have charisma, more than others close to me – and yet you have a lack, a vast hole I can fill.'

He stares at me: a warrior brings him some accoutrements, silently he fits them on. I say, 'It's a technique – away of sorting out your memory, you put it all in rows ...' and I think, but do not say, 'of onions' – 'Experiences too – there's no more random. It is all controlled. This memory garden will protect you from the unforeseen – the past that you forget, that bursts back like a weed.'

MacTaggart says, 'Thank you so much,' but he's quite unprepared. I say,

'I've looked quite carefully – your storehouse. And your project – the choice of friends who'll then become your enemies and suffer terribly. And seek revenge ... The end – it's all in the beginning ...'

'Look,' he says, 'my friend. This is a dump, the guys are all quite poor. I give them soldiering, I take a little cash,' and on he goes. I say,

'I know. It's quite banal. Yes, there is a vision, but it doesn't make the light.' He shakes his head. I take it he agrees.

*

I say to Candy, 'I know nothing of your life. Or Marlin,' and she says,

'You're quite inquisitive for once. It makes me smile – usually, your box is good enough, it holds your life inside...'

'Well?' I say. 'That's what it's all about, our lives.'

'Mine – you know, it's fleeting. Vows. Our great project. It's a stone. Now, that's enough for you! We're not MacTaggart – he needs lots of life, and people's lives, to tip the balance.'

*

'Here, the tunnel ends,' I say. 'Just place this nitro charge. MacTaggart never blew himself right through, with all that metal, they just advanced so far and doubled back ... the compass went askew.'

We make the blast. The mountainside again, and down below, another airport. People who come and go.

'That small MacTaggart,' Candy says, 'someone will kill him, that's for sure. One of his important friends ... Those are the best. First you are useful, then you're not. Then, you're a pain. I see it all, it's like those maps of places no one's been, you fill them up with fantasies, and in due time, you find you're right – the monsters are all there, and things you'd not invent, as well. My! How the present weighs – the future too, it's even heavier.' She sighs, and I say,

'It's the flying does it – your body moves, your spirit's left behind.'

*

If it's still there, to home we go.

Here's Marlin: 'I've been watching you, of course. Now I expect you want a narrative, that makes some sense of all the roaming you have done.'

'Yes, yes,' we cry. 'A map, the roads that go from there to here, politics, economy, lay it all in rows.'

'Well,' Marlin says. 'One murder, quite confirmed: one recruit – still doubtful. A revolution scarcely baked, a warlord with fine boots – it isn't much, but here it's even worse.'

We look over at the sheds – there is a hologram, memorial. It's Marlin on his back and overpowered, fighting some brainy porridge on the lawn. Now, we see the silver roof is buckled back, those bronze doors, with their scenes of Ramayana, tales of the Shahs – oh no, the artistry is bulged and cracked, they couldn't be insured ... The key was lost ...

'I let them out,' Marlin lies. 'The next scene is, bacteria that rule the world. I hoped they'd scuttle down the drains – instead, they went off chanting to the woods.'

'They have voices, opera?' I ask.

'More of a hum. And every opera together, all at once. My! but they're brainy – into that forest, and they trashed the restaurant, it seems the menu pleased. They grow and grow,' and he cries out. 'Too soon, too soon. That crap – it should come after, when we cannot see – and now, who knows, it maybe rules the world, and we can't know what are its goals, its rules: oh, stupid us!'

'And the dragons?' Candy asks.

'A disappointment,' Marlin says. 'If you wish, you'll walk them. They are small and tame, their breath lukewarm, libido less than nought.'

*

My plans – a great success. I took the boss's girl, I didn't do my job. I am commander of the whole. But – all that, it doesn't satisfy ...

Candy says, 'My brother, when we left ...'

Marlin replies, 'Brother? Maybe he went to look for you. To find out where he is. That backing singer, now –

music is a trade that sets you up and casts you down, maybe she too went looking for you, or found a cave in Chad and an unhappy life ... Maybe they found each other, singer, brother, and lie unhappy in each others' arms, and wish the sea would come and bear them both away, and drift up in an unknown place, and there you are, Candy and you, by chance you're walking on the sand – there's always sand – and there, you think it is a fish, a shell, a dolphin suicide. But no, it is your two loves, a trace of red, a rag of dress on one – and there's a breath, two mouths that come apart and say your names, and "where am I, where are we? – upthrown and wrecked, and at the mercy of some Robinson, some tribe of circus-makers, looking for some freaks, or master chef to serve us up, with parsley in our orifices, seaweed-draped, or grey and foetal on a board, with salt rubbed in, still pulsing, postcoital, singing a song of mermaids, of the cold blue deeps where shelves of nearly-living stuff lifts with the tide, and dreams of light..."'

'They are both lost?' I ask.

'To me, and probably to them,' says Marlin, with satisfaction.

'My little murder, Marlin dear?' asks Candy, coyly.

'I saw it all,' says Marlin with anguish. 'Your infidelity, with Dum and Dee and Doe and Jane and Joe, the traitors all, and risking life and fame. And how you took against that guy, Khalid, and told him of Macbeth, and tricky snicks with knives, and how he could be king, but mind the forest – and he said, "Lady, here there are no trees, even the wardrobe's made of bronze on silver struts, a wondrous thing," and how you had your sexy way that overdid the cuts and thrusts. He dies – and bundle him in golden cloth, myrrh in his eyes and out his guts, and mummify him there and hope his mates will put him in some chamber, stay a thousand years, until the tourists come and put him under glaze. How they will speculate! I love hypotheses, as you both know,' he says, a dream comes to his face and pauses there, 'But maybe knowing's even better ...'

'And holding it against me,' Candy says, making her voice small, contrite.

*

'Candy, you aren't worth a spit,' he says.

'How can I speak of fine things,' asks Marlin, 'When you two go stamping through the world, its terror, its beliefs – the sounds, explosions, mutinies ...? And what can save us? What could ever save? Surely, we see the signs, apocalypses; the mountain slides, its molten core exposed – look! how the animals go skittering down the slopes, the birds are fried in air. Are we so stupid we don't see? – at best, there's not a reasoning malign, great spirit of the self-destruct, we sacrifice ourselves to please it ... who would say it thinks of pleasure, or of justice, pity? – all it knows is passion, can't recognise a drama or a consequence ... Death of the beloved – what a torment, what a joke ... And at the worst? It's really much the same, a toss of the invisible dice, your number's always coming up, but you can't see the spots. You just sit on at the table, all those hands, they tweak and tug – at the start, they give you money, then you lose, you suffer every loss as though your stake was earned, the cash pulls out like nails, with blood and slime attached, until it's gone, all gone. And at the end, you are pathetic. Smile a rictus, not noble in your underwear – they are all around, the good examples, sweet old things demented. Little ignorant ones who sing a song...'

'Stop, stop!' cries Candy. 'Yes, I betrayed, but don't deserve this twirl, this dance of death of all,' and Marlin says, 'What? Wasn't this what it was all about, the things you don't deserve, and here they are? You want an either-or? Things happens all the same, whether you follow pleasure or Macbeth – quite uncaring, down it comes, the forest doddering on its roots, just like the movies show. Or it's perhaps the killer mud, indifference to good and bad, sloth and endeavour – aliens in pods like moths or bees, or else invisible, a virus or a madness, implants beneath the skin – laboratory tricks or actors who're unseen, not unionised, and of course unpaid ...'

*

The wood, that restaurant ... the scene, the horror – sealed, wrapped in the wardrobe, drama folded like a rose still furled, a bud – and in due time we'll see the petals crack apart. Still odourless, the plot still thick.

'Stop this,' says Candy. 'We've heard it all before – the dice, the game. It's not your case, it's just your riff – the money rushes in, you needn't stir, or even kiss the bones...'

'You've heard it all, oh yes, but now you've done it: some for the first time,' says Marlin. 'Besides, now I'm just a rich – a very rich – young guy. My bugs have gone. Science and genius too. With us, now, without the bugs, the world – what you can hear and see and smell, the rosy-fingered dawn, the wine-dark sea, all that, the mermaids and the pigs, the loyal dog, the snooty bride – all that is done! It's finished. Cognition takes a different track, and – hail to the boss! the new lord species! Listen to the bugs! – "we're hungry now for silver, dig and dig, and melt down every glint on every skeleton we find". The path has changed. New world. It's bugs' eye level that we're at – perhaps the moon is purple and the sky is green, the earth a copper slab – now, up the steps they drag the sacrificial viruses, and there's some lord of misery with sixteen legs, a nucleus of raspberry jam, that's waiting for the show of faith and love ... All that, you'll never know, you'll never see.'

We listen, sometimes smiling, sometimes – a tear, for all we'll miss, or all we've missed, and Candy says,

'There is some blame for you. You let us roam, you made a mess of science. That was arrogant.' She'd go on, but Marlin says,

'No crime, no blame. I can't say that for you.'

‘This guy,’ and Candy points to me, she tries to save my day, ‘Our general, we’ll have him sleep inside – a rug, maybe, beside our bed, or even curling loyally on top ...’ but Marlin says,

‘No, no, he sleeps outside. Now I am merely rich, and very rich, I need some bodyguards – the rich, like me, they all have those. There’s sure to be some guys, now that the sheds is empty, that come to steal the roofs. Those guys with shotguns – where’d they finish up? There’s good stuff in those sheds, and artistry. Those doors ... We need some guards to sleep inside, and bear whatever brunt ...’

I say, ‘The guards, they must be Zoroastrians – they are the very best.’

‘So be it, then,’ he says. ‘Now, I’ll return to your disasters: failure to check my mail, the genius squandered as you stumbled down the stony paths, followed some warriors, their freedom flags, the scrabbling in the shale,’ and on he goes.

*

I think, there must be blame for him, or else we’re left alone with nothing but Khalid, and guilt – like those old Greeks who never had a moment in their life forgetful of the corpse, abduction, incest, desecration of some grove or casual screwing of a nymphet skipping down the track ... He must be guilty like the rest, can’t just take the cash, and on and on, the science and the reason quite traduced – without a fault, without remorse ...

'Marlin, there's blame,' says Candy. 'You let our species down.'

'Nonsense,' says Marlin. I say,

'You let the hotstuffs out – you should have kept them in, until there was no longer hope for us,' and Marlin says,

'They just got out. Not my idea. No blame. That's life.'

I say, 'Suppose they eat us – that should leave some blame. It's like the Trojan War all over,' and Marlin laughs,

'Your movie's crap. Besides, they're not carnivorous.'

'They never had the choice,' says Candy, 'Think of those poor fish – that restaurant, as the bugs rampage,' and Marlin's angry, and he says,

'It only happens in a script. They just rolled off, and no one's going after them,' and that is true for all of us, and Marlin criticises us some more.

'Marlin, all this, it is not trivial,' I say.

'Khalid is done with,' he says. 'Stabbed in sexplay. He's just a hold I have on Candy now. Lust, that's her trouble. Luxuria. Every time she takes a trip, she trips. My sin is pride, Superbia, so it takes a little time to win me back.'

He's in command again. He says,

'Those guys – those with MacTaggart. Let them leave their goats, desert the poor – that's typical of all of us. I shall call him Tagger, drop the folklore or the pseudonym. It seems that guys of his religious bent can be hired for terror, revolution or security, on level terms. Between these three, these missions, there's connect. For now, it's bodyguards I want, and he can get some groups of guys that's similar, signed up around the world. My net. The search for genius, the postcards – that takes second place for now. I feel like Frankenstein – now my invention's running wild, I think Idea time is up! I need those guys' protection. There's an empty shed that sleeps fifteen, they'll start off there.'

And so they do.

*

Tagger brings his loyal men.

'They'll tag our enemies around the world – around the ankle,' Marlin says. 'We'll have a list, a billion names will do, and tags to match,' and so the project starts.

I say, 'I'm still attached to postcards, and my backing singer too,' but Marlin scoffs – 'They'll not go back to Chad, that group – guys there have music of their own. Think of the song and not the singer,' but it doesn't satisfy.

Tagger says they're Zoroastrians if required. Besides, religion's now banal, it's civic virtue that we need. Religion doesn't mobilise, and so security's the task, but Marlin says a guy must have a faith.

We start to build again.

'This shed's a kind of baptistery, beyond my house,' says Marlin: 'We need to modify, of course. The monkeys on the doors – those we'll replace with goats. Inside, an altar, guarded every night and day.'

That silver roof exploded back – it's like a sardine-can unrolled, the contents – bugs – gone roistering off, and knocking Marlin down and burning as they went. We heave the metal flat again. It's polished slick and cleaned by sort-of mouths, and guys retool the bronze: out with the monkeys, in the goats, for old times' sake. We lay the marble on the floor, the green and black, and then we chisel in a hint of brawn and salmon to the stone, that chimes poetically with bugs gone by and moving on. And in the midst we plant the flame.

*

The fire altar. With its guardians, angel-types, on either side the flames, with swords and rods – or Candy's stick. A stick – quite ceremonious. More potent than a sword.

Marlin says, 'The shifts will be arranged, but for a start, it's you and Candy for a week or two. Now, take good care – the flame must stay alive, remember, and my bodyguards will come to you and do whatever they decide to do. Pray, shout or meditate, or other things – it's up to them.'

But they don't come, perhaps don't know the rituals, and we stand there like idiots for days and nights. I miss my candle flame you didn't need to tend. I think of singers, and the harvest – pomegranates, redder than the fire, and sweeter too.

We're not believers. I'm employed, possessed: Candy atones.

'I guess this is our punishment,' I say, and Candy says,

'I guess your sin is mediocrity, you can't say that of me. The punishment is always at the last, when all's been done and justified. But – I can live with this ...' and if I can't, that is too bad, the fire needs two, and so I stand and stare – my sword: the flame: and Candy's stick. No weapon, but her wand, a ritual tool that brings immunity. Behind – a shape that must be Candy too, unless she's paid some guy to do her shift. Immunity?

*

'I'm clean again,' she says. 'On with the new. The trick has worked. Might be this stick – or else, it's prudence, and being loyal to Marlin.'

'What a mind,' I think, and say, 'My only sin's complicity, there is no punishment for that, it's in the air, the soil, the birds, the worms, it's what we live by, and we die in it.'

But Marlin says, 'Idleness, that's what. That is your sin, and sins must be washed off,' and in the roofs there's tubes, and if he's in a righteous mood, he flushes me, and there's the fire to light again.

I think, 'Goddam these military roads, the trudging and the standing still, attention without ease, and everyone converted into soldiery and cleaning boots and standing guard and planting bombs or dropping them ...'

Candy says, 'My! You're banal! You, Marlin too, is that the best your search for genius can do, some commonplace about the wars, the peace, that creaky wheel: the doors that never close, our species struggling? Prostrate and begging – "water", "land" "the right", "the wrong".' On she goes, the world will end its ways before she ends her song.

I say, 'My dear – your comments: even more banal!' and then she laughs, that's true, she says, and what a pity Khalid couldn't play her game – although I think he maybe played it all too well.

'Well, what's your point?' asks Candy. 'If one you have. You want the new, and that means war: then you want peace. My points would be: accept what you think you see – and wow! circling the world, we turned up some odd stones! Go deeper, always. There's more stones. Follow your instinct. Follow your boss. Do you want a cuddle? – for old acquaintance, as they say.'

'If there's no knives,' I say, joking.

'Only a fling, that was,' she laughs. Over her breasts, in silver thread embroidered: '*tant pis*'.

Sweaters, she must have hundreds, sayings too.

'Now I must go back upstairs to him,' she says.

And so she does.

Tagger marches his warriors, up and down. They find it hard to keep in step, but military life's moved on since that was all the latest thing.

Go deeper, you avoid old Franco, stuck on his surfaces, civilisations swirling by, with no mark left.

Or – there's harvesting the pomegranates. Idiocy of rural life.

Deeper and deeper. Look! there, down the hill, gently down ... no grass, no birds. You see the wood ... all tingling with life.

## About the author

John Fraser has lived in Rome since 1980. Previously, he worked in England and Canada.

www.ingramcontent.com/pod-product-compliance
Lightning Source LLC
Chambersburg PA
CBHW020550310726
48979CB00008B/1164/J
* 9 7 8 0 9 5 6 9 0 9 8 6 2 *